MONSTERS

UNLEASHED

JOHN KLOEPFER

ILLUSTRATED BY
MARK OLIVER

HARPER
An Imprint of HarperCollinsPublishers

Monsters Unleashed

Copyright © 2017 by Alloy Entertainment and John Kloepfer

All rights reserved. Printed in the United States of America.

No part of this book may be used or reproduced in any manner whatsoever

without written permission except in the case of brief quotations embodied

in critical articles and reviews. For information address HarperCollins

Children's Books, a division of HarperCollins Publishers, 195 Broadway,

New York, NY 10007.

www.harpercollinschildrens.com

Library of Congress Control Number: 2016053472

ISBN 978-0-06-229030-4 (trade bdg.)

Typography by Aurora Parlagreco

17 18 19 20 21   CG/LSCH   10 9 8 7 6 5 4 3 2 1

First Edition

For my beautiful wife, Jenny —J. K.

For the Rohanoceros —M. O.

1

The day was gray and cloudy, and the air felt steamy and soupy. Sitting in art class, Freddie Liddle felt like he was living inside the pressure cooker his dad used to make his world infamous, way-too-spicy chili.

Freddie sighed. His dad's cooking just reminded him of his mom and how she used to make him normal dinners before his parents got divorced.

Which reminded him of moving to this hot New Mexico town.

Which only reminded him that he was the new kid.

Which reminded him of the bullies constantly tormenting him.

Which made him wish he could disappear.

And that just reminded him that as a six-foot-four-inch sixth grader, being invisible was pretty much impossible.

Squeezed into the tiny seat in front of his easel, Freddie glanced around the room at his twelve-year-old tormentors. Unfortunately, art class was the one class of the day when they were all together. There was Jordan, the super athlete; Nina, the popular girl; and Quincy, the mega-nerd. They looked like normal kids on the outside, but beneath the surface they were . . .

Monsters.

If it wasn't for his best (and only) friend, Manny Vasquez, Freddie might have been the loneliest kid in New Mexico.

A sharp screech from the art room's loudspeaker interrupted Freddie's thoughts, as Principal Worst's voice rang out from above: "Attention all sixth and seventh grade soccer players. Due to a faulty sprinkler system, the field is flooded with mud and unfit for play. The soccer game will be rescheduled at a later date."

Jordan Cross, the biggest jock and the biggest jerk at school, twisted up his face, angry and confused. "Are you freakin' kidding me? My game is canceled!"

Freddie made the mistake of making eye contact with Jordan. Something about Jordan's glare always made Freddie freeze up, stiff as a statue.

"What are you staring at, Gigantor?" Jordan said. "Did you have something to do with it?"

Freddie flicked his eyes away and twisted uncomfortably in his tiny seat.

"You probably tripped and fell and caused an earthquake and that's what screwed up the sprinklers . . . ," Jordan said.

Quincy and Nina laughed and gave each other a fist bump. The only thing these two had in common was hating on Freddie.

Manny looked up from his self-portrait. "Hey, why don't you guys lay off my boy; go down to the cafeteria; talk to my girl Carol, the lunch lady; and get yourself a nice tall glass of shut up."

Freddie chuckled to himself. Manny never backed

down from anybody, no matter how much bigger they were than him. And at four foot seven, pretty much everyone was bigger than Manny.

"Learn to take a joke, bro," Jordan said.

"I think in order for it to be a joke, it has to be funny," Manny shot back.

From across the room, their teacher, Mr. Snoozer, shushed them in his monotone voice. "Everyone please focus on their self-portraits for the remainder of the class. . . ."

Freddie tried to shrink away, but it was no use. He *was* gigantic just like Jordan always liked to remind him.

So instead of working on his self-portrait, Freddie pulled out his sketchbook, where he had drawn Jordan, Nina, and Quincy's inner monsters—the horrible creatures he imagined lurked inside each of them. Anytime they were mean to Freddie, instead of talking back, he just opened the book and added another detail to his creations. For having hands the size of baseball mitts, Freddie's fingers were surprisingly nimble.

Manny peeked over Freddie's shoulder as his big

4

buddy sketched. "Looking good, Freddie! Our movie's going to be awesome once we 3D print those guys."

Freddie and Manny's movie, *Manfredo Lives*, was set in the future with radioactive mutant monsters roaming the wasteland. Their main character, Manfredo, is the last boy on earth and has to fight three different monsters and defeat them all.

Mr. Snoozer looked up from his desk and addressed the class. "For those of you hoping to 3D print today, I'm sorry but they sent us the wrong printer, so we won't be printing anything anytime soon."

"But, Mr. Snoozer! You promised," Manny said.

"Mr. Vasquez, please don't start with me today," Mr. Snoozer replied.

"This stinks like toe jam on a hot day!" Manny whispered. "Now we can't shoot our movie."

Freddie frowned as he put his monster notebook away and turned back to his self-portrait. Well, it was sort of a self-portrait. It was actually a painting of a fluffy, big-bellied, three-armed creature with two tusks and two horns named Oddo. Freddie was almost done with it and, not to brag, but it was pretty dang good.

SPLAT!

A spitball landed in the middle of Freddie's drawing.

"Bull's-eye!" Jordan celebrated.

Nina started laughing when she saw the wad of soggy paper dribbling down Oddo's face. Quincy chuckled as well.

Freddie picked off the spitball and wiped his fingers

on the side of his jeans. It wasn't worth fighting back. They'd just pick on him some more. That was that.

Or so he thought.

Freddie watched in awe as Manny flung the tip of his paintbrush in Jordan's direction. Paint splattered *everywhere*. All over Jordan's clothes, the floor, the walls.

Jordan's nostrils flared as he got up and shoved Manny back as hard as he could. Manny flew into Freddie, and Freddie fell over Nina, knocking her easel over in a domino effect. Quincy's easel tipped as a chorus of high-pitched *oohs* came from the rest of the class. Quincy and Nina's paintings both crashed to the floor, along with dirty brushes and murky paint water.

"Hey!" Mr. Snoozer stepped in. "Manny and Freddie, thank you very much for giving up your recess period so you can clean this mess up. . . ."

"Aw, man! But that's no fair!" Manny whined. "Jordan started it!"

"But you finished it," Snoozer boomed. "And unless you want to stay after school, too, I suggest you find a mop."

The bell rang just then, signaling the end of class. Freddie and Manny both hung their heads, staring down at the floor while the rest of the class, including Mr. Snoozer, headed off to recess. They looked around the art room. *What a mess*, Freddie thought.

With everyone else at recess, Freddie attempted to dry his drawings with an old hair dryer from last week's papier-mâché project. The paper was a little wet and crumpled, but the drawings weren't smudged. Freddie was relieved. He stared at the three creatures, reviewing the list of their features.

There had been a rumor going around that Quincy's retainer could pick up Wi-Fi signals. That was how Quincy had never gotten less than an A+ on an assignment. Of course this wasn't true, but sometimes Freddie wondered. How else could the kid know *everything*?

Manny sidled up next to Freddie, holding a mop. "This would go a lot quicker if *two* people were cleaning. . . ." Then he saw what Freddie was looking at. "Yo, if these are your only copies, we better print these suckers before something else happens," he said.

"We're already in enough trouble, Manny," Freddie said in a worried tone. "And besides, Snoozer said they sent the wrong 3D printer."

"Adults lie all the time," Manny replied, holding up the damp drawing of Kraydon. "Like when my mom says she forgot to buy chocolate ice cream but really she just buries it in the back of the freezer under the frozen peas and broccoli."

Freddie just shrugged in response. They finished cleaning until the lunch bell rang, making Freddie jump at the too-loud *brrrring*. Through the window, the boys saw the rest of their classmates filing in from the school yard. Freddie's stomach grumbled loudly.

"Maybe we should print them later?" he said. "It *is* sloppy joe day."

"No one's around! Snoozer's probably on his second sloppy joe already. Now's the perfect time," Manny said. "Come on."

"Okay, okay, I guess sloppy joes can wait . . . ," Freddie said, lumbering after his little pal with his notebook.

They snuck into Snoozer's office. On the desk, connected to the computer, was a strange-looking machine, shaped like a rounded cube with kind of a pyramid point on top of it.

"There it is . . . ," Manny uttered in a hushed whisper. It looked different from a normal 3D printer.

"Snoozer was right. This printer looks superweird," said Freddie. "Maybe we should hold off. . . ."

"How different can it be? You press print and it lasers plastic into the shape you want," Manny said. "Boom. Simple." He had done his research.

On Mr. Snoozer's shelf was a ripped-open cardboard box marked "3D Printer Supplies." Manny reached in the box and pulled out a see-through plastic cartridge filled with a weird pinkish blob. It looked like the speckled bologna-like mystery meat that they served in the cafeteria. He threw the box back on the shelf, and an avalanche of small packets labeled Silica/Desiccant: DO NOT EAT fell on the floor at his feet.

"Watch it, man!" Freddie grumbled.

"Well, don't just stand there!" Manny pushed the keyboard toward his friend.

"Okay, okay." Freddie booted up Mr. Snoozer's computer and opened an app called Sculptris. He knew how to use the program already because they'd been practicing in art class, just never with a real printer. Snoozer's computer lit up with a bluish-white glow as the program popped on the screen.

"Hurry," Manny whispered. "The Snoozmeister could be back any minute."

"I know what I'm doing," Freddie replied. He laid his notebook facedown on the scanner. The 3D printing software mapped the drawing, and Kraydon appeared on the screen. Kraydon had two enormous arms; muscles rippling with tough, scaly skin; and a single eye in the center of its face, like a Cyclops.

Freddie took a deep breath and scanned the next drawing.

Yapzilla was covered in sleek black hair, like Nina's, and had two long headless necks sprouting from her middle. At the end of each neck was a mouth, one to breathe fire, the other to let out a deafening screech.

Freddie double-clicked on the third scan. Mega-Q popped up—a creepy part lizard, part millipede with razor-sharp legs and arms like a praying mantis. Freddie and Manny quickly loaded a cartridge of pink goo into the machine. Freddie hunched over the computer and selected all three files to print. "Here we go. . . ." He smashed his finger down on the print button.

The 3D printer hummed to life. The pinkish goo drizzled from the printer, creating the first monster— Kraydon.

The boys watched, wide-eyed and smiling, as the machine worked its 3D magic. Every detail from Freddie's drawing printed to perfection.

Freddie picked up the six-inch tall monster and studied it. Kraydon was smushy like gummi candy and stretchy like Silly Putty.

He turned the little ball of monster in his hand and

moved his arms around a bit. "He looks so real!" Freddie exclaimed, as he poked the minimonster in the tummy with his index finger.

Then with a tiny growl, Kraydon's eye popped open.

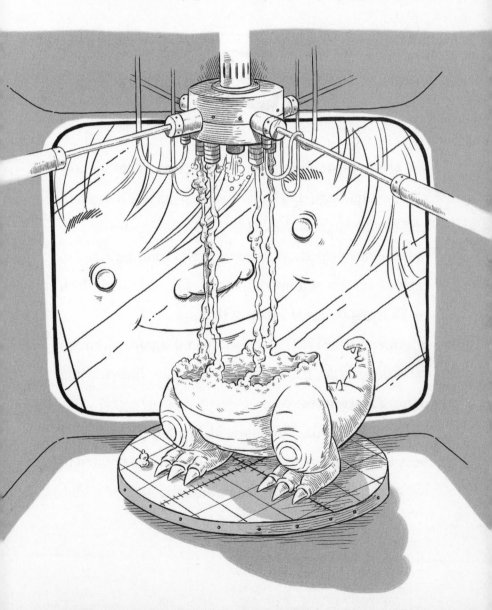

The boys stood in stunned silence as the little monster's eyelid started to blink. Kraydon opened his mouth and croaked again. *"KROOAAAAARRK!"*

Freddie yelped and dropped the monster on the table. Kraydon scampered across Mr. Snoozer's desk on all fours and growled up at the boys.

"KRAAAAAYR!" Kraydon roared again, although he was so little, it almost sounded cute, like a kitten doing a lion impression.

"Hey, little fella," Freddie said, bending down. "Don't be scared. My name's Freddie, Fred-dee!" He pointed to his friend. "That's Manny, Man-knee!"

Kraydon snarled and backed away to the edge of the desk.

Suddenly, Kraydon's eyeball began to swirl. A pulse of energy shot out of the monster's pupil.

The ray beam rippled through the air and hit an

apple on Mr. Snoozer's desk. The apple turned into a hunk of gray rock.

Freddie's mind was swimming. His teachers always

said he had an "active imagination" (which he knew was their nice way of saying he was a weirdo), but could he be imagining this? Freddie shook his head vigorously from side to side to make certain he wasn't seeing things, but he wasn't. Kraydon was still right there in front of them.

This was really happening.

Another pulse emanated from the minibeast's eyeball. But this time Kraydon was looking right at Freddie and Manny.

"*AHH!*" The boys yelled as they dodged the pulse, which struck the mirror on the back of Snoozer's door. The beam bounced off the mirror and hit one of the silica packets from the 3D printer's shipping box. The packet turned gray and hardened to stone, too.

Kraydon swung his club-like tail and smashed down hard on the little sack of Do Not Eat pellets. They exploded in a small burst of rocky fragments.

"Whoa!" Manny yelped and ducked under the desk.

Freddie put his hands up and started talking to the little monster. "J-just chill out, man, I mean, monster. We want to be your friends. . . ." He spoke softly, as if Kraydon were a puppy.

In a quick burst of energy, Manny lunged for Kraydon. The minimonster dodged the sneak attack, running over the computer keyboard, hitting almost every key before leaping off the desk.

As the little monster hit the floor, the 3D printer beeped to life. Kraydon raced past Freddie's feet and shot through the office doorway.

The boys chased the monster back into the art studio. "Go that way!" Manny ordered Freddie to one side of the classroom while he went to the other side. They approached the tiny beast slowly,

trying to corral him, but Kraydon was too small and fast.

Behind them, the 3D printer bleeped and wonked. The machine was drizzling goo into the forms of

Freddie's two other monster drawings: Yapzilla (Nina) and Mega-Q (Quincy).

"Oh shoot!" Freddie shouted.

"Go turn that thing off!" Manny shouted to Freddie. "Before it's too late!"

Freddie spun around and caught his foot in the legs of an easel. He tripped, knocking over a shelf of art supplies. The place looked even worse than before they cleaned it up.

Kraydon stared up at Manny, his teeny-tiny nostrils flaring as he grunted.

"This little dude's not getting away from me again . . . ," Manny said, cornering Kraydon near the paint-splattered sink. "You're about to get got."

As Freddie scrambled to his feet, the overhead lights started to flicker.

"Come here, you little troublemaker," Manny whispered, moving toward the critter.

As Freddie reached the doorway to Snoozer's office, the printer went berserk. Sparks flew from the electrical outlet, traveling up the power cord, and sending smoke out of the machine. The 3D printer rattled and let out a loud BEEP!

Then the power shut off completely.

The lights blacked out and everything went dark, except for a rectangular patch of dim daylight coming in through the window. They heard the *crunch-splat* of something dropping to the floor, then another *crunch-splat*. Freddie stared in shock as two new little monsters stepped out of the shadows into sunlight.

Yapzilla's eyes darted back and forth, looking around

the room. A thin blue volt of electricity zigzagged between the sluglike stalks protruding from Mega-Q's head.

Freddie was speechless.

But Manny was not.

"Holy freakin' crudballs!" he exclaimed. "They're alive, too!"

Kraydon's tiny roar bellowed through the classroom and the floor trembled.

Suddenly it didn't sound so tiny.

The boys had been so distracted by Yapzilla and Mega-Q that they'd forgotten about Kraydon. The monster was now standing in a puddle next to the sink. Its skin soaked up the paint water, swelling like a sponge. In a matter of seconds, Kraydon had doubled in size.

He was now as big as a pug puppy. A very angry, very dangerous-looking pug puppy.

"Did he just . . . *grow*?" Manny asked.

"Uh-huh! He just sucked that puddle up like his skin

was made of straws!" Freddie exclaimed, still in shock. He couldn't believe this was really happening!

The muscle monster took off running. Manny took off after him, trying to snatch him up, but the little monster juked to the right. Manny slipped on the wet floor and went flying forward as the little critter scampered out of reach. Full steam ahead, Kraydon bashed through the base of the art room door and left a jagged hole in his wake.

Meanwhile, Freddie ran toward Yapzilla and Mega-Q. They scurried across his path, and he squealed as he tried to sidestep the newborn critters, so as not to trample them. Freddie toppled to the ground with a thud, as

Yapzilla and Mega-Q escaped through the hole, too.

"We have to get them back!" Freddie yelled, clambering to his feet.

The boys darted into the dark, empty hallway after the monsters. The lights were off throughout the entire middle school. Freddie could hear banging coming from the basement as the janitors worked to get the electricity back on.

As they rushed down the hall, one of the doors flew open and Mr. McLaughlin, who taught seventh grade English, stuck out his head, hollering after the boys. "Slow down, wouldya?"

But they couldn't.

They ran past the double doors where the rest of their class was scarfing down their sloppy joes in the half-lit cafeteria. The kids didn't seem to mind eating in the dark. They could hear the teacher on lunch duty telling everyone to stay calm, assuring them that the lights would be back on shortly.

Freddie and Manny slowed down as they caught a whiff of the delicious smells wafting out of the dining

hall. They looked down the length of the hallway. Their monsters were nowhere in sight. "Where'd they go?" Manny asked. Freddie shrugged, and they raced on, stopping at the intersection of another hallway. Then a flash of motion caught their attention. At the far end of the empty hall, they spotted their trio of 3D-printed monsters galloping into the science room.

"Come on!" Freddie said as they ran into Mrs. Fletcher's science class. "They went in here!"

Manny used the flashlight on his phone to light up the shadows in the classroom.

"You see them?" Freddie asked in a whisper.

"There!" Manny shined the flashlight on the table.

All three of the monsters were climbing up toward the aquarium full of fish.

"They can't get wet!" Manny yelled.

Freddie rushed through the rows of tables and stools and reached his long arms across the table. He scooped

27

Yapzilla and Mega-Q away from the fish tank.

"Gotcha!" he said with a whoot. He dropped the wriggling creatures into the pockets of Manny's cargo shorts. Then Freddie opened the front pocket of his backpack, planning to trap Kraydon. But the one-eyed muscle ball scuttled away and smashed the aquarium with his tail.

Water spilled through the cracks in the glass and a wave washed across the table. Freddie swiped for the monster, but Kraydon was too quick and disappeared out of view, jumping down onto the wet floor and scampering through the shards of broken aquarium glass.

Manny whipped around the flashlight, frantically trying to find the monster, when they heard Kraydon smash another hole through the bottom of the door.

This jagged hole was bigger than the last one.

"He's getting away!" Manny said. "After him!"

"Wait," Freddie said, looking down at a fish flopping on the floor. "Help me."

"Oh, come on," Manny said. "It's just a bunch of fish. They don't even have feelings."

"That's not true! I had a fish once, and he had feelings!" Freddie said. "Get some water."

Manny grunted, then quickly filled a beaker with water at the sink. The two boys plucked up the squiggling fish off the floor by their slimy tails and dropped them in the water.

"There, are you happy now?" Manny said, and took off, Freddie close behind.

They jetted back into the hallway and skidded around a corner. Kraydon was nowhere in sight. They sprinted down the next hall, back past the cafeteria.

"Hold it, boys!" Principal Worst suddenly called out.

Freddie and Manny hit the brakes. The principal's high heels clacked loudly as she approached behind them. "Freddie Liddle and Manny Vasquez . . . ," she said slowly in a slight singsong voice. They knew they'd been caught.

Freddie's pulse thumped like a drumbeat as they turned around to face the music.

A hand-in-the-cookie-jar look crossed Freddie's face as he gazed down at Principal Worst. *We're totally busted*, he thought, freaking out. Manny, however, seemed chill and relaxed, or as Manny would say, *chillaxed*.

"Hey, Mrs. W.," he said, making casual conversation. "When are the lights coming back on?"

"Soon, I hope, but my bigger concern is why you're running in the halls," she replied, her arms crossed.

Brghrurgh! A weird grumbling noise came from Manny's pockets.

"What was that?" the principal asked, eyeing Manny suspiciously.

Freddie tensed up, his nerves jangling.

"That?" Manny said, suddenly clutching his stomach. "That's the sloppy joes talking. You know how it is. So good going in . . . so bad going out."

"Yeah, that's why we were running . . . ," Freddie added, holding his own belly with a pained look on his face.

Principal Worst stared at them hard for a long moment. "Tummy troubles, eh?"

But they had bigger troubles than make-believe indigestion. Behind Principal Worst, Freddie could see Kraydon waddling down the hallway like some sort of mutant penguin.

He watched as the monster pushed through the swinging door of the boys' bathroom.

"What are you looking at, Freddie?" Principal Worst turned around. "Who's there?"

Freddie shrugged dumbly. Just then, the lights suddenly flicked back on, bathing them in bright white fluorescence. *Saved!* Freddie thought.

"Please," Manny said, clutching his tummy again. "It's an emergency. . . ."

Their principal stared at them for a couple of seconds longer. "Okay," she said. "I'll give you a pass, but this is strike two. . . . One more and you're out. . . ."

"We're really sorry," said Freddie. "It won't happen again."

As Principal Worst walked away, Freddie and Manny made a beeline for the bathroom. Freddie felt his blood pumping. *That was a close one!*

Now inside the boys' bathroom, Manny peeked under the row of stalls for any feet (human or otherwise). "All clear!" he shouted.

Freddie flung open the door to the last stall, a big

handicap stall at the end.

There was Kraydon, crouched against the wall behind the toilet, trying to hide.

"There he is!" Freddie gasped. He dropped to his knees and spread his arms wide, pinning the little monster in the corner. Kraydon made a dash for it, but Freddie snatched up the creature before he could escape again.

"Finally." He sighed as Kraydon squirmed in Freddie's big mitts.

Then the monster's eyeball started to swirl again.

"Watch out!" Manny swooped in with some toilet paper and wrapped it around the monster's eye. The toilet paper turned to stone, solidifying around Kraydon's

Cyclops eye. Freddie stashed the writhing, blindfolded monster in his backpack and got to his feet.

"Manny," Freddie said, "I think we have to tell someone about what's going on."

"No, we don't," Manny said. "Didn't you just hear what Principal Worst said? Two strikes . . . you really want a third? They'll call our parents. We might even get suspended!"

"We just created monsters from a 3D printer!" Freddie said. "This is some serious high-level, top-secret stuff going on!'

"How do you know it's high-level or top secret?" Manny asked.

"We just created three living, fire-breathing, and whatever-elsing monsters with a 3D printer!" Freddie shouted. "You don't think that's insane?"

"Keep your voice down," Manny said, looking around, all paranoid.

"Sorry . . . ," Freddie whispered.

"You're right, you're right." Manny looked down at the linoleum floor. But when he looked back up, he waggled his eyebrows up and down. "But think how cool they are going to be for our movie!"

"What? Manny, that's crazy." Freddie shook his head. "We need to tell the police. The FBI. The CIA. NASA. The . . . the . . . whoever deals with monsters department?"

"We will, we will," Manny said, his voice smooth like cheese dip. "Just as soon as we've trained them to act and we've shot our action scenes."

Freddie had to admit the idea was appealing. He pictured their monster movie in his head. If they *could* train the monsters to do their own stunts, they might really have something special on their hands. And if they made the first-ever movie with real-life monsters, well, maybe he wouldn't just be known as the gigantic freak. He'd be known for making the monster blockbuster of the year.

"Fine," Freddie agreed, calming down a bit. "Deal. But we have to start training them right away."

"Deal . . . ," Manny said and put out his hand.

As Manny and Freddie clasped their hands together, two feet dropped to the floor in the stall next to them.

Feet that were wearing a pair of jangling cowboy boots. Boots that could only belong to one person.

The stall door flew open with a sharp bang, and Quincy Moorehead stepped out.

"Well, well, well . . . ," the evil mega-nerd said, tapping his fingertips together, *pit-a-pat, pit-a-pat*. "What have we here?"

Freddie and Manny froze in the center of the boys' bathroom. The overhead lights hummed in the silence. Freddie's backpack went crazy as Kraydon wriggled around inside. Manny's cargo pockets were jumping like they were filled with angry hamsters.

"What are you two up to?" Quincy asked, squinting at Freddie and Manny.

Manny found his voice first. "We were actually having an AB conversation, so why don't you C your way out of it."

"Monsters, eh?" Quincy continued. "I hope this isn't some kind of prank. The last kid who tried to pull a prank on me, well, let's just say it did not go so well for him or his little science camp project."

Freddie gulped, a hard swallow. They had to get out of here before this evil kid genius figured out what they'd done.

Then with a sudden whoosh, Manny's pant leg went up in flames. A thin tendril of smoke rose to the ceiling, circling the smoke detector. It began to beep.

"Yo!" Freddie cried. "Your shorts!"

Beep. Beep. Beep.

Manny looked down at his pants and squealed. "I'm on fire!" He smacked his thigh with an open palm to put out the flames. "Ouch, ouch, ouch!" A small yap and another puff of smoke wafted from Manny's scorched pocket. The smoke rose and hit the smoke detector again. The beeping got louder and the fire sprinklers clicked on, spritzing water everywhere. Freddie reached up on his tiptoes and tried to unscrew the smoke detector from the ceiling.

But it was too late. The three of them were already

soaking wet from the indoor downpour.

"Oh, for crying out loud," Quincy snarled. "I knew this was a prank!"

"Quick, Manny, we have to get them out of here!" Freddie yelled. "The water makes 'em grow!" Freddie spun his pack around so that he was covering Kraydon from the sprinklers. But as he rushed to the door, it was flung open in his face.

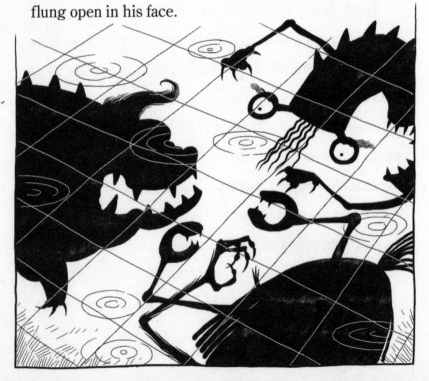

Jordan Cross stumbled into the bathroom, lurching past Freddie. He was cupping his stomach with both hands, his face knotted with pain and anguish.

"Too many sloppies," he groaned. "Wait, why is it raining in here?" Jordan looked up in confusion at the sprinkling sprinklers.

SKCRRREHK!

A rip sounded from Manny's pants as Mega-Q's razor-sharp legs poked through the fabric, slicing it to shreds. Yapzilla tore through the tattered threads and burst seams of the other pocket with her talons.

KAK! KAK! KAK! The metal teeth on Freddie's backpack zipper popped as Kraydon crawled out and scrabbled down Freddie's chest, waist, and legs, hopping off the toe of his big sneaker and onto the bathroom tiles. The little monster swung his tail around his body and struck himself in the face, smashing the stone blindfold that covered his eyeball.

"Monsters on the loose!" Manny yelled, running after their creations.

Quincy was in total shock, his mouth hanging open,

his hair dripping wet. "You made monsters. . . . How did you . . . ? How is that . . . ?"

The now not-so-little critters ran across the sopping-wet floor, between Jordan's feet, and into the hallway.

"Don't let them get away!" Freddie shouted. "After them!"

But the monsters were too quick. Freddie and Manny chased after the monsters as fast as they could, trying not to lose sight of them.

"Come on!" Quincy said, slapping Jordan on the back.

Mega-Q led the way into the gym, with Yapzilla and Kraydon following the lightning-fast millipede.

The boys raced through the double doors and sprinted across the basketball court. "Where'd they go?" Manny asked, looking around in a panic.

"I don't see them . . . ," Freddie replied.

"This is insane, even for you guys," Jordan grumbled behind them.

They came to a stop in front of the double doors that led to the swimming pool. Freddie's heart sank. He knew exactly where the monsters were.

Screams rang out through the chlorine-scented air, and Nina burst out of the pool room, shrieking at the top of her lungs.

Jordan ran up to her, and shaking her by the shoulders, he ordered her to chill.

"You chill!" she snapped. "There are monsters in the swimming pool!"

"What are you doing in the pool?" Quincy asked her. "You're supposed to be at lunch."

"Well, if you must know, I prefer the

swimming pool bathroom to the regular bathroom," Nina said, talking fast. "Plus the girls' bathroom is all filled—it's sloppy joe day. But that's not the point right now, 'cuz the swimming pool is full of monsters!"

"They're in the pool?" Manny asked, his voice filled with panicked nerves. "In the water?!"

Freddie and Manny looked at each other, their eyeballs bulging.

Just then, the loudspeaker pierced the air with a high-pitched screech and Principal Worst's voice blared: "This is not a test! This is an emergency evacuation! Everyone stay calm and make your way outside in an orderly fash— Holy Mary, mother of monsters—" The announcement cut off.

Manny looked confused. "How does Principal Worst know about the monsters?"

"Because they have security cameras in the pool area," Quincy replied. "Duh!"

"Don't 'duh' me, dummy . . . ," Manny snapped.

"I can say 'duh' whenever I want," said Quincy. "It's a free country!"

"I'm gonna duh-ump you both in the pool with those monsters if you two don't shut up," Jordan said.

A mad scramble of locker clanks and door slams

and squeaky sneakers and shrieking squealers echoed through the gym as everyone rushed to leave the building. The emergency bell blared.

This was not good.

This is actually very, very bad, Freddie thought as he and Manny and the two other boys moved cautiously across the gym toward the swimming pool.

"What are you guys doing?" Nina shouted. "We have to get out of here!"

"We just want to see," Manny said. "They're our monst—I mean, they're monsters!"

"Ugh . . . boys. Fine, let's get a look, then we're out of here." Nina groaned and followed after them.

Together, the five classmates crept through the doors of the pool room.

Freddie could see the three monsters shimmering beneath the surface of the water. They were growing bigger and bigger as the water level of the pool sank lower and lower. Then the monsters rose out of the deep end.

Kraydon was as big as an elephant.

Yapzilla was the size of a giraffe.

And Mega-Q was as long as an anaconda.

For the first time in his life, Freddie felt as small as a mouse.

KRUARHHHHHHH! Kraydon roared and lifted his massive fists, smashing them down on the pool deck. The ceramic tiles cracked and crumbled under his weight. All five of the kids were backed into a corner, their eyes bugging out of their skulls.

"Freddie! What do we do?" Manny asked, terrified.

One of Yapzilla's necks pointed and aimed directly at them. The she monster pursed her lips and spat a stream of fire.

Freddie dove out of the way and scrambled back to his feet, slipping and sliding on the deck. Mega-Q reared up on his hindmost legs. A neon-blue bolt of electricity shot out at the kids.

"Watch out!" yelped Freddie.

"Retreat!" Quincy shouted, and the five of them scurried back into the gym.

BZZZT! The door crackled with blue electricity and then fizzled out.

Freddie was in shock. Everything had started out so harmlessly. All he'd wanted to do was make a little monster movie.

Now the monsters were destroying his school.

BAM! BAM! BAM!

Freddie peeked back into the pool room through the circular window above the door. He watched as Kraydon swung his spiky tail and smashed a giant hole through the wall that led to the playground. Mega-Q and Yapzilla escaped through the hole. The runaway monsters darted across the school yard and through the parking lot, disappearing in a whirlwind of electrified fire.

"Dude, this is so messed up!" Freddie said. He slid down the gym wall and sank his head in his hands. "Dude, what are we supposed to do? This is all our fault, dude!"

"Calm down, take a deep breath," Manny told him. "And stop saying 'dude' so much." He pulled Freddie aside from the bullies, who were huddled together in a corner of the gym. "Now, let's just think. How are we going to stop these monsters?"

"How should I know?" Freddie sputtered. "Just because I designed them doesn't mean I *understand* them."

"That's it!" Manny jumped up. "I think I know what we have to do."

"You do?" Freddie asked. "What is it?"

"I'm your best friend," he said. "You trust me, right?"

"Yeah, yeah, yeah," Freddie said. "What's your idea?"

"Know thy enemy . . . ," said Manny.

"Huh?" Freddie asked, looking down at him oddly.

"Know. Thy. Enemy. It's like basic strategy," said Manny. "The only way to defeat your enemies is to understand the way they think. That way you can know their strengths and weaknesses."

"You want to ask *these jerks* for help?" Freddie whispered in sheer disbelief.

"Yes, okay, they're jerks," Manny said. "But your monsters are based on those three jerks. . . ."

"I don't know about this, Manny. . . ." Freddie shook his head uncertainly.

"I don't like it any more than you do," said Manny. "But we have to face it. It takes a bully to fight a bully."

Freddie grumbled under his breath. Manny had a point. Maybe Jordan and Nina and Quincy *could* understand the monsters better than he and Manny could. Maybe if they teamed up together, they could stop the monsters before they destroyed the town. It wasn't a sure bet, but at least five heads were better than two . . . even if those heads belonged to Jordan Cross, Nina Green, and Quincy Moorehead.

The bullies had climbed up on the bleachers to look at the monsters through the high gym windows. Manny and Freddie shimmied up the wooden steps and stood behind them. Yapzilla was clomping through the school yard, setting the playground ablaze with her flame-thrower breath. Mega-Q was coiled around a telephone pole, snipping the wires with his razor-edged front legs.

Freddie couldn't see Kraydon.

"Where'd the third one go?" Jordan asked. "The big one?" He turned to Freddie. "Why isn't it with the other two?"

"Well, funny you should ask . . ." Freddie cleared his throat anxiously. "So, umm . . . these monsters are based on the three of you. . . ." He let that hang there for a sec.

"What are you talking about—'based on us'?" Jordan asked sharply.

"Show them the drawings," Manny said.

Freddie dug around in his backpack and pulled out his sketchbook.

"There are monsters on the loose!" Nina screeched. "We don't have time for some stupid drawings!"

Freddie did his best to ignore her and flipped through his sketchbook. With a shaky hand, he opened it up to the monstrous versions of the sixth grade's three biggest bullies, the same bullies standing right in front of him.

"That's you . . . ," Freddie mumbled to Nina, pointing out the window at the two-headed monster, then down at his drawing. "You're Yapzilla."

"That's the me monster?" she asked, perplexed. "Why am I called Yapzilla?"

"Because you never shut your yapper," Manny jumped in. "And also you're two-faced."

Nina gasped, totally offended.

Quincy pointed to the picture of Mega-Q. "And I suppose that nasty-looking millipede fellow is me?"

"Uh-huh," Freddie said.

BOOM! The bleachers shook as the gymnasium wall split open with a giant crack. A spray of cement and plaster exploded as Kraydon's tail came crashing through. Freddie watched in horror as the massive beast climbed through the jagged hole. Kraydon paused in the cloud of white plaster dust where the doors to the pool used to be.

Quickly, the kids dropped from the top of the bleachers and hid underneath the wooden steps. The giant beast lumbered slowly onto the basketball court, scanning the gym with his gigantic Cyclops eyeball.

"And that thing—?" Jordan asked, with almost a tremble in his voice.

"I think it's the you monster," said Nina.

"Yup." Freddie squinted through the slats of the wooden bleacher seats. "That's the you monster."

Quincy scratched his head in confusion as Kraydon grunted and punched a hole in the hardwood floor. "How did your monster drawings become real actual monsters?"

Freddie took a deep breath. "You guys were being really mean, so I drew these monsters to show what you look like on the inside. . . . We tried to 3D print them for our movie, and then somehow they came to life."

"You're making a movie?" said Nina.

"We *were* making a monster movie," Freddie said.

"Oh really?" Nina asked skeptically. "Do you have an agent?"

"No . . ."

"What about a producer?"

"No . . ."

"Then it's not a real movie," she said.

"It's a real movie if we make it . . . ," Manny said.

Nina made a face. "I don't think so. And I would know. I'm going to be famous."

"There isn't going to be any movie," Freddie interrupted. "Not anymore."

"There isn't?" Manny said. "Why not?"

"Because we're about to get eaten by real monsters!"

Kraydon's tail swatted the floor dangerously close to their hiding place under the bleachers. They waited in terrified silence as Kraydon sniffed the air and grunted. The monster's mouth opened wide and he let out a deep bellowing roar. Kraydon turned around and dug his claws into the floorboards, splintering the gym floor.

"So now what?" Jordan whispered.

"We have to work together and stop the monsters," Freddie said. "Because the monsters are based on you, only you can help stop them . . . we think."

"That's a terrible hypothesis," Quincy said.

"You got a better one?" Manny asked. "We created those things, but you're the only ones who really know them."

Nina crossed her arms. "Why should we help you?"

Manny rolled his eyes and threw up his arms. *Only the meanest kids on the planet wouldn't want to help save the world*, Freddie thought. But that was no surprise—that's how this whole mess had started in the first place.

"The only reason I drew those pictures was because you guys never stopped picking on me," Freddie said. "This is on all of us, not just me and Manny."

"Oh, that's so typical," Quincy said. "Blaming everyone else for your problems."

"All I'm saying is I really wasn't planning on getting killed today," Nina said.

"Yeah, no duh," said Manny. "None of us were."

"Well, maybe you should have thought about that

before you whipped up a bunch of monsters," Quincy snapped.

"How were we supposed to know that weird printer was going to print out real monsters?" Freddie asked, staring down at his three archenemies.

"And now you want to be monster hunters . . . ," Nina said.

"Yes," Manny said. "And we need your guys' help. . . ."

"I got news for you little nerd bombers," Jordan jumped in. "You're not monster hunters!"

Freddie didn't appreciate being called names, but Jordan was right. Just looking through the wooden bleacher seats at the monster in the middle of the gymnasium, he knew they weren't the ones hunting the monster.

They were the hunted.

Kraydon's bloodcurdling howl tore through the air as the monster prowled around the gym. There was no way they could escape. They had to stay put. From their bleacher hideout they listened to the sound of the buses revving up and vrooming off. The rest of the school had gotten away. Now it was just them against the monster.

Gulp. Freddie tried to swallow his fear.

"Great, we missed our chance to get away," Nina said quietly. "I just want to say that if I die, and don't win an Oscar, that it's one hundred percent all your faults. . . ."

"Shhhh!" Manny shushed her with a finger to his lips, and she shot him a death stare.

"Freddie, you're the one who designed this thing," Quincy whispered. "Does it have any weaknesses?"

"Probably not," Jordan chimed in. "If it was designed after me."

Manny rolled his eyes at the jock.

"He's right," Freddie conceded. "It's nothing but a big ball of superstrength."

"So, basically indestructible," Quincy said.

"And pretty destructive . . . ," Freddie added.

Kraydon was now at the top of the three-point line. The monster's eye swirled clockwise and pulsated.

"Wait, look . . . ," Nina interrupted. "It's doing something weird with its eye."

"Oh yeah, that's one of his powers, too," Freddie said sheepishly. "His eyeball can turn stuff to stone."

"Great," Nina replied. "This keeps getting better!"

Kraydon aimed his gaze at one of the basketball hoops. His eye swirled and shot out a blinding beam of energy, turning the whole thing—backboard, rim, and net—to stone. The monster leaped off his hind legs and smashed the backboard to bits in a violent slam dunk. It

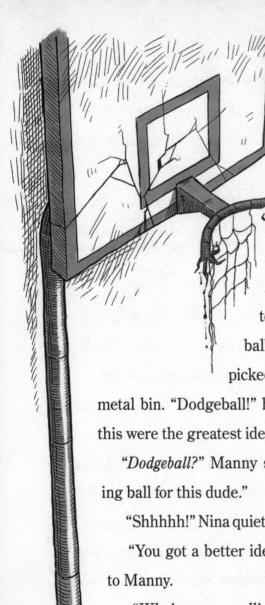

seemed like all the monster wanted to do was destroy every single thing in sight.

Jordan sneaked out from under the bleachers and squatted behind a blue metal ball bin. "I have an idea!" He picked up a few balls from the metal bin. "Dodgeball!" he whisper shouted as if this were the greatest idea of all time.

"*Dodgeball?*" Manny said. "We need a wrecking ball for this dude."

"Shhhhh!" Nina quieted them a little too loudly.

"You got a better idea, Chump?" Jordan said to Manny.

"Who're you calling a chump, Chump?" Manny retorted.

"I call them like I see them, Chump," Jordan muttered.

"Chumps! I mean, guys!" Freddie said. "Chill out! He's gonna hear us!"

Jordan and Manny stared at each other, sneering. Jordan made a move toward Manny like he wanted to throw down. Manny backed away and Jordan knocked the metal bin with a clang in the quiet gym.

The monster whirled around with a thunderous stomp.

"I'll make a distraction to cover you while you guys make a run for it," Jordan said bravely, grabbing a few more balls out of the bin.

"On your mark," Freddie said. "Get set . . ."

"Go!" Nina shouted, and the four of them sprinted out from under the bleachers as Jordan hurled a red bouncy ball at Kraydon's face. Kraydon galloped toward the bleachers and charged at Jordan, who dove out of the way, firing another ball.

The monster roared angrily as another ball nailed him in the chest.

"You're out, bro!" Jordan cried, but it was clear that this monster didn't follow rules.

Kraydon whipped around at the four others trying to escape. Freddie, the biggest and slowest of the bunch, jumped over a heap of rubble from the smashed-in wall. He huffed and puffed, running with everything he had. Manny high-stepped around a hole that was circled by the thick, sharp shards of the floorboards, next to Nina and Quincy. The monster's eyeball swirled at them again, and a pulse of blue light zinged across the basket-ball court.

Jordan launched another ball. It sailed through the air and struck Kraydon square in the eyeball. BOING!

As the ball blasted the monstrous creature, Freddie, Manny, Nina, and Quincy hustled through the doors of the gym, spilling and toppling over one another into the hallway. Kraydon shook his head and blinked his eye a few times, dazed from the hit.

Jordan sprinted after the rest of the group. "Woo-hoo!" he yelped. "You see that? Got 'im good!"

"Got him nice and angry is what you did . . . ," Manny said. "Look!"

Freddie peered back over his shoulder. Kraydon was charging at them, ripping up the hardwood floor with every giant step. His claw pierced the red skin of a ball and popped it as he galloped across the court.

The kids scrambled out of the monster's path, pawing at one another, desperate to get away. Behind them, there was a door at the end of the hall. At the other end, daylight spilled through the glass of an emergency-exit door.

Kraydon skidded to a stop on the sideline. The wood

floor rippled up like a wave, shooting splinters in every direction as the monster barreled into the double doors. WHAM! Kraydon's arm smashed through the hallway wall. The monster's head and shoulders were in front of them, blocking their escape route to the exit.

Kraydon let out a bellowing snarl, his stinky breath hitting the kids as they backed away from him, toward the door at the end of the hall. The monster tried to squeeze himself fully into the hallway but couldn't get through. He was wedged in the doorframe!

Freddie exhaled a sigh of relief. They were safe—at least for the next ten seconds.

Kraydon jerked and wriggled, fighting to jam his too-big body through the door. His mouth slime streaked through the air, splattering across the front of Nina's shirt.

"Are you kidding me right now?" Nina scowled and paused to inspect her clothes. "I got this at Val's Vintage. It's one of a kind. . . ."

"Why? Because it's been worn by a previous owner?" Quincy said snootily.

"If you knew anything about fashion, your opinion might actually matter to me," she said. "Have you even looked in a mirror lately?"

"Oh yeah? Well I'm rubber and you're glue—whatever you say bounces off me and sticks to you," Quincy said.

Freddie surveyed the hallway as Quincy and Nina argued. Jordan had stopped paying attention and was looking at his reflection in the glass of the trophy case. Jordan had more than a dozen supershiny trophies in Gallup Middle School's Hall of Fame already. The monster was less than ten feet away, blocking the hallway and their escape to the front of the

school, and Jordan was fixing his hair and flexing his muscles.

Is he really that vain? Freddie wondered, when all of a sudden, Kraydon's arm broke through the rubble of the demolished wall.

SNAP! KACHUNK!

"Jordan, look out!" Freddie cried as Kraydon's claw shot into the hallway, swiping back and forth like a giant cat pawing at a mouse in a mousehole.

Kraydon's arm crashed into the trophy case, shattering the glass and knocking the awards to the floor.

Jordan's eyes crossed in anger. "No one hurts my trophies!" the jock yelled in a fit of rage. As he charged at Kraydon, the monster flung out his arm and threw Jordan against the wall. With a thunk, Jordan hit the wall and went limp, sliding down to the floor in a slumped heap.

Just then something clicked in Freddie's mind. His thoughts flashed back to when Mr. Snoozer's apple had turned to stone, and then to Nina and Quincy's bickering: "Whatever you say bounces off me and sticks to you." And finally he looked at the jock sprawled on the floor with his beloved trophies.

Freddie sprang into action, hurrying over to the shattered case. He grabbed a shiny trophy off the shelf and wielded it with both hands.

He gripped the trophy and shielded Jordan from the monster's gaze just as Kraydon's eyes spun. The monster's eye beam bounced right back at Kraydon and hit him square in the face. Freddie held the deflected beam on the monster.

But nothing happened.

Kraydon just snarled and growled, still stuck in the doorway. The ferocious brute shifted his weight back onto one foot then lunged forward. His claws tore away the walls, and Kraydon wriggled his whole body down the hall, his back scrunched down but still scraping the ceiling.

Nina and Quincy rushed over to Jordan and dragged him out of Kraydon's reach.

"Come on!" Manny shouted from their end of the hallway. "Down here!"

"Come on, come on!" Quincy yelled, holding the basement door open.

Kraydon crawled toward them, snarling and snapping his ugly teeth. Jordan rose to his feet and shook the cobwebs out of his head. He followed the rest of them down into the basement. The monster's chomping mouth filled the entire hallway as Freddie slammed the door shut at the top of the staircase.

At the bottom of the narrow basement stairwell, Freddie breathed a quick sigh of relief: the monster was way too big to cram itself down the staircase. But from the thunderous boom rumbling the ceiling it sounded like Kraydon was trying to pound his way through the floor above them.

"Do you think if we stay down here, he'll go away?" Manny asked.

"I don't think so," Jordan said, while stretching his back. "If this monster's anything like me, he's going to keep coming at us until he gets what he wants."

"What's that?" Nina asked.

"To turn us into statues and then smash the statues to smithereens," Freddie said.

"Ugh, why'd you have to make him such a psycho?" she said.

"Because *he* is a psycho . . . ," Freddie replied, pointing to Jordan.

"Watch it." Jordan glared at Freddie.

"So what's the plan? How do we stop him?" Quincy asked. "Now that Manny has so brilliantly trapped us in the basement."

"I do have a plan, thank you very much," Manny replied. "Watching Freddie fight Kraydon gave me an idea, but we gotta gear up."

"What do we need?" Nina asked.

"Anything with a mirror," Freddie told them, knowing exactly what his little buddy was thinking. "'I'm rubber and you're glue. Whatever you say bounces off me and sticks to you!'"

"Exactly." Manny nodded and ripped the mirrored door off a medicine cabinet in the janitor's bathroom.

"I get it," Quincy said slowly. "That's smart, actually. We're going to use Kraydon's power against him. When he shoots his eye laser at us, we'll use the mirror to reflect it back at him."

"And if he's anything like Jordan, he's going to love looking at himself in the mirror," Manny finished.

"Exactly," Freddie confirmed. "But he can't turn himself into stone. I already tried that."

"We're going to have to lure him and get him stuck somewhere . . . ," Quincy said, thinking out loud.

"What about the flooded soccer field!" Freddie said.

"Not bad," said Quincy. "When he shoots out his eye beam, we can bounce it right back at the mud. The mud will turn into cement and he'll be stuck good."

Nina, Quincy, and Jordan all started rummaging around the cluttered equipment room.

"Look at this!" Nina ran over to a storage bin and started pulling out a tangled mass of orange soccer nets. "We could use these," she said. "Lay them on top of the mud. Tangle him all up."

"Yeah!" Manny said. "I always get snaggled up in those things."

"We'll need a diversion to get him in position," Quincy added.

Jordan rummaged in the equipment bin and found a megaphone. "That'll be me," he said. *"Everybody get in position,"* he said into the megaphone. It screeched loudly, and they heard Kraydon stomp around upstairs.

"Dude, put that thing away, will ya?" Freddie said, clasping his hands to his ears. "Are you trying to get us all killed?"

"Okay, okay," Jordan said. "Sorry. Chill out, Gigantor."

"Can you please not call me that?" Freddie asked timidly.

"Whatever, Gigantor," Jordan said. "Didn't know you were so sensitive."

"Come on, you guys," Quincy said. "Let's get out of here before that thing figures out how to get down here."

Quickly, the five of them grabbed their gear and lugged it up the other stairwell toward the exit. Jordan opened the door slowly, and they stepped outside behind the school building. The coast seemed to be clear. *Maybe Kraydon got bored and wandered off*, Freddie thought. They strained to hear his booming footsteps, but the air was oddly silent.

Then as they neared the soccer fields, they could hear Kraydon's thumping on the other side of the school. They passed a parked car. Jordan dashed forward and kicked off the side view mirrors. "I always wanted to do that," he said, and tossed one of the mirrors to Quincy.

The nerd bully fumbled and nearly dropped it on the cement. "You almost just got me seven years' bad luck!" He glowered at Jordan.

"You caught it, didn't you?" Jordan replied. "So what's the big deal?"

"Come on, guys," Freddie said. "We have to focus." He tried to sound like a leader, but his voice was meek.

"If I'm not back with a monster in five minutes," Jordan said, stretching out his legs in a runner's lunge, "just wait a little longer."

The group nodded, and Jordan ran off to look for Kraydon. Freddie, Manny, Nina, and Quincy dragged the soccer nets out to the field. Freddie stepped into the muddy grass, and his feet sank into the soil past his ankles. If they could trick Kraydon into turning the mud into cement, the monster would be stuck tight.

It wasn't long before the four of them managed to set the trap.

Now all they had to do was wait. They tromped back through the mud and hid behind a row of cars parked at the edge of the school's lot.

In the distance, they could hear Jordan yelling into the megaphone. "Hey, you! Yeah I'm talking to you, you big ugly ball of muscle!"

Suddenly, Jordan came sprinting around the corner of the school, the monster fast on his heels. Kraydon gained on him, faster and faster. Jordan stopped on a dime and dove out of the way, right before he hit the soccer field. Kraydon was too big to slow down in time, and they all watched as the massive beast slipped and slid through the mud, right into the middle of the field.

Brown muck sprayed everywhere as Kraydon's tail hammered the muddy turf.

"Get ready!" Freddie shouted.

The monster growled in surprise as his feet tangled in the soccer nets and he sank deeper into the mud.

It's now or never, thought Freddie. He jumped out, waving the trophy in front of Kraydon's scaly face. The monster looked down at him, his sharp teeth bared in a slimy grin. Freddie gulped nervously. He normally wasn't this brave.

Kraydon became an-
grier and angrier that he
couldn't reach the trophy,
despite his strength. His
eye started to pulse, getting ready to shoot out his
stony gaze.

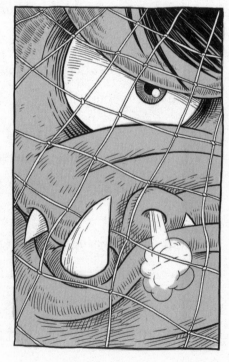

With a roar, Kraydon
shot a pulse from his swirling eye, aimed straight for
Freddie.

At that second, Manny sidled next to Freddie with the janitor's mirror.

"A little help, please!" Manny called out. The rest of the kids held up their mirrored objects like shields, too, inching closer to the mud-covered beast.

"We're doing it, buddy!" Manny shouted to Freddie.

"Hold it steady, guys!" Freddie yelled as the monster's pulsating gaze deflected off their mirrors. "Couple more seconds!"

Freddie planted his feet in the mud and held up the trophy with all his strength. This time, the energy pulse from Kraydon's eyeball was more powerful than Freddie expected. It was as if the angrier Kraydon was, the stronger his power became. Freddie struggled to hold on to the trophy, praying that the metal wouldn't crack under the pressure.

The mud hardened around Kraydon's massive front paws, back legs, and tail, trapping the monster in place.

Before Kraydon knew what had happened, he was stuck tight, like a toy soldier with his feet connected to a plastic stand. The monster's eyeball stopped swirling.

Kraydon strained with all his might, trying to break out of the stone slab around his tail and feet. Suddenly, the tail broke free and rose, swinging over their heads.

"Look out!" Nina shouted.

"Heads up!" Manny cried.

They dove out of the way as the tail came crashing down. Kraydon kept swinging his tail, trying to crack the cement encasing his legs, but it was useless. The monster couldn't smash himself free.

Kraydon let out a defeated roar.

"We did it!" Jordan, Nina, and Quincy all yelled out at the exact same time.

"Ahem." Manny cleared his throat. "I think you mean, *he* did it," he said, pointing to Freddie.

"I hate to admit it," Quincy said, pointing to the cement holding Kraydon in place, "but it was a pretty *solid* plan . . . pun intended."

The kids gathered around Freddie, and Quincy gave him a high five. He felt ten feet tall. Normally, that would not be a good thing, but today it absolutely was. "It was a team effort . . . ," Freddie said seriously.

"Yeah, but if it weren't for your plan, we might all be bits of rubble right now," Nina said, patting him on the back. "Way to go."

"The plan wasn't all his . . . ," Jordan butted in. "I kinda helped a lot. . . ."

"You were awesome, Jordan," Freddie said. "The plan wouldn't have worked without you."

Jordan looked up at Freddie. "You weren't so bad yourself, Gigant—I mean, big guy. . . ." Jordan put his hand out for a high five. "Good work, man!"

Freddie couldn't remember the last time he'd heard those words, *good work*. And he'd *never* heard them from Jordan Cross.

"You're going to leave me hanging?" Jordan said, with his hand still in the air.

"This is just the first time you've been nice to me . . . like ever," Freddie said hesitantly as he slapped Jordan's hand. "Any of you," he said, looking at Nina and Quincy.

"Well, you finally did something good," Nina chimed in. "You keep doing stuff like this and I just might remember you when I get superfamous."

"We all did our part," Manny said excitedly. "Maybe we're going to be monster hunters after all."

Suddenly, a high-pitched screech howled through the air. The wail of fire truck sirens whooped in the distance. Yapzilla was out there somewhere, wreaking havoc with her shrieking and fire breath. They could hear the faint sounds of panicked yelling from their neighbors and the squeals and honks of cars as everyone rushed to get out of their monster-ridden town.

Freddie thought about his dad and Manny's mom and the rest of their classmates and teachers. He prayed they were okay. The kids had to take down Yapzilla and Mega-Q quickly, before things got even more out of control.

"We're not done yet. . . . We need a plan for the rest of these monsters," Freddie continued.

"I think it's time to call in the big guns," Manny said.

"What do you mean, big guns?" Nina asked.

"You know, like the military, marines, army, navy SEALs, the National Guard, everyone!" Manny said. "NATO, FBI, CIA, NSA, MIA..."

"MIA?" Freddie asked.

"Monster Intelligence Agency," Manny joked.

"Great idea," Freddie said. "How do we do that?"

Manny led them back through the school, heading for the principal's office. The gymnasium walls were completely caved in. Student artwork, posters, and bulletin boards were scattered in the rubble. Kraydon's arms had left giant dents in the lockers, and a huge claw mark scarred the walls. Gallup Middle School was completely destroyed.

They ducked into Principal Worst's office at the front of the building.

"There should be a hotline or something . . . ," Quincy said.

Nina pulled out her cell phone. "No service. . . ."

"Try the landline," Quincy ordered.

Jordan picked up the phone and listened for a dial tone. "The phones are dead."

Freddie reached up to flip on the television that hung in the corner of the ceiling. "TV's out, too."

"Mega-Q was clipping the wires," Quincy said. "He must have been cutting off our communication."

Manny clacked the keyboard, trying to get online. "The internet's down, you guys!"

Nina pinched her chin in serious thought. "If we can't get in touch with anyone else, it looks like we're going to have to do this on our own. . . . After all, we do understand our monsters better than anyone."

Freddie looked at his three biggest enemies in the whole wide world. Except now they weren't his enemies . . . they were his partners. He felt like he could trust them. It was kind of nice having them on his side for a change. Together, they had brought down Kraydon. They could definitely take out Yapzilla and Mega-Q.

Couldn't they?

"Let's do this thing," Jordan shouted.

"Let's go kick some monster butt," said Nina.

"Technically speaking, I'm not sure your monster has a butt," Quincy said.

"You know what I mean," Nina said.

"Let's go!" Manny shouted, leading the charge.

And with that, they were off to save their town from the rampaging monsters they had created.

The sixth grade monster hunters left their half-demolished school and scanned the landscape. "Where are they?" Nina asked.

The desert surrounding their town was mostly flat. There weren't a whole lot of places for the monsters to hide. Except for the main strip, the place was nothing but chain-link fences and stretches of endless telephone wires. It wasn't very pretty to most people, but Freddie wasn't like most people. He could find something cool in what everyone else thought was ugly.

Freddie refocused on the task at hand. He spotted two dark tendrils of smoke rising from the center of town. *Yapzilla.*

"Check it out, over there!" Manny pointed west on the horizon. "Yapzilla must be setting the whole town on fire!"

"That looks like it's near the news station," Nina said. "I bet that's where she's going!"

"Why would she be going there?" Quincy asked, a bit snippily.

"Because if she's anything like me, she probably has a *burning* desire to be on TV," Nina replied. "Yapzilla wants to be a monster star—like Godzilla!"

The kids grabbed some abandoned bikes from the lot in front of their school and in less than ten minutes, they had reached Aztec Street in the center of town. The

air smelled like burned rubber, and the street was completely deserted. A lone police cruiser sat silent on the corner. Its lights flashed, and its doors were wide open. Everyone must be hiding from the monsters.

Even the cops, Freddie thought.

It was all too quiet and eerie. The sky had grown heavy and dark. It looked like a rainstorm could be on the way. Things felt tense, like the moment before the big battle in a video game. *Except this movie is real*, Freddie reminded himself.

They pedaled down an alley and passed a Dumpster. The heavy metal lid lifted and some guy's head popped out.

"Don't go that way," the man said, "unless you want to get flame broiled by a two-headed squawk monster." He closed the lid back down over himself.

"Wait!" Freddie said, looking at the end of the alley. "Which way is the TV station?"

From inside the Dumpster, the man's voice said, "Left, I think . . ."

The kids reached the end of the alley and peered around the corner. They saw the TV station in the distance.

"What else do we know about her?" Quincy asked.

"She's basically a two-headed beast that breathes

fire out of one head and lets out a supersonic screech from the other," said Freddie.

"A screeching, fire-breathing monster?" Quincy said. "Are we sure we want to do this?" He slowed down on his bike.

"Come on, guys. We just took down the biggest, baddest, and might I even say handsomest of the monsters," said Jordan. "A two-headed fire breather shouldn't be a problem. We just need our strength!" He pulled out a bag of beef jerky from his pocket and started to stuff his face with the freeze-dried meat.

"Where'd you get that from?" Freddie asked.

"At school," Jordan said, talking with his mouth full. "They just started selling it in the vending machine. They have all three flavors. You want some?" he asked, offering the bag to Freddie.

"Are you kidding?" Freddie said. "I'm practically made of the stuff." Freddie's mouth started to water as he reached for the jerky.

"Psych . . . ," Jordan said, pulling the bag away from him.

Freddie hung his head.

"I'm just messing with you," Jordan said, and let Freddie grab a handful of the dry, salty beef.

Freddie stuffed his mouth with the beef jerky. "Thanks . . . I'm starving. . . ."

"Stop!" Jordan said, grabbing Freddie by the wrist. "Don't eat that!"

Freddie looked down, expecting Jordan to be pranking him again, but instead he saw a little packet of silica pellets mixed in with the beef jerky. Jordan plucked it out and threw it on the ground. "Dude, that stuff will mess you up."

"Okay, jerky boys," Nina said, interrupting their beef jerky bonding as they arrived at the station. "We're here. Time to rock and roll." They ditched their bikes and headed inside.

SCRRREEEEEEEECH!!!!

Their eardrums rattled as they entered the TV station. The monster's shriek carried through the hallways like a sonic wind.

SCRRREEEEEEEECH!!!!

The kids all covered their ears. Freddie plugged his fingers into his earholes as far as they would go.

"You guys, we're going to need some actual earplugs or something if we're going to stop her," Freddie yelled over the monster's scream. The noise was unbearable.

With their fingers jammed in their ears, they moved deeper into the empty TV station. The place looked like it had been abandoned in the middle of the news broadcast. Cameras were still pointed at the stage, ready to shoot, lights blaring on set.

The two-headed monster came back into view and the kids ducked through a door marked with a sign: Goodie Room. They looked around and realized that this was where the TV station kept all their giveaway prizes. The kids dug around for anything that might help them against Yapzilla.

"Got it!" Nina held up a box of brand-new noise-canceling headsets.

"But if we're all wearing these headphones, won't it be hard to hear each other?" Freddie asked.

"Yeah, how are we supposed to communicate?"

Jordan asked. "My basketball coach always says good communication is the key to winning."

"I may have a solution," Quincy said as he pulled out a box of walkie-talkies.

They covered their ears with the headphones. Freddie cranked up the volume while Quincy tuned the walkie-talkies to the same channel.

"The headsets are now connected to the walkies," Quincy explained. "Now we can all hear each other while blocking out the screech."

Freddie was impressed. He could hardly hear Yapzilla's screech anymore, but Quincy's voice was crystal clear.

"The glorious results of three summers at Northwest Horizons science camp." Quincy smiled. "Man, you think *monsters* are weird, you should have seen what I saw *there*," Quincy muttered under his breath.

Looking around, Freddie couldn't believe he was in this mess. But he wasn't sure what was stranger—going into battle against some 3D-printed monsters or battling them with his worst enemies. Well, *enemies* was a strong word. But . . . friends? Were these bullies turning out to be his friends?

"Okay, what's the plan?" Freddie whispered, coming back to reality.

Nina looked at him. "If Yapzilla wants to be famous, let's make her think she's famous."

"That doesn't sound like much of a plan," Manny said as they all moved slowly down the narrow corridor of the news station.

"Trust me," Nina said, walking in a crouch. "I got this."

They peered out the door and saw Yapzilla lurking on the stage. She wasn't quite as huge as Kraydon was, but she was still fairly large. Her body was about the size of a Volkswagen Beetle, and she stood on two enormous ostrich legs. Her twin necks protruded from her hair-covered body, and each one ended in a mouth, one for screeching and one for breathing fire. She had to duck her necks down so she wouldn't knock her mouths on the ceiling.

The monster stepped into the camera frame and saw her image on-screen. She yipped happily, then blasted the monitor with her fire breath.

Nina backed up in fear and turned to the boys. "Maybe I don't got this!"

Manny grabbed her by the shoulders and looked her in the eye. "You're an actress, right? You just have to go out there and play the part. Don't even think about it. Just improvise."

Nina paused, took a deep breath, cleared her throat, then conjured up a look of intense focus. "'What a to-do to die today, at a minute or two to two'"; she spoke the

words as fast as she could. "'A thing distinctly hard to say, but harder still to do. We'll beat a tattoo, at twenty to two, a rat-tat-tat-tat-tat-tat tat-tat-tattoo, and the dragon will come when he hears the drum at a minute or two to two today, at a minute or two to two.'"

"What the heck was that?" Manny asked.

"My vocal warm-up," she said and picked up a microphone off the floor. She looked out at the she monster. "I'm ready for my close-up. . . ."

"I think you may have just created a monster, little buddy," Freddie said to Manny.

"No, big buddy," he said. "That would be you."

Nina adjusted her headset and clutched the microphone tightly in her hand. "Okay, boys, I'm going in," she said. "Wish me luck."

Nina took a deep breath and stepped confidently onto the stage. Freddie snuck behind the set and climbed up a narrow ladder to the gridiron walkway hanging above the studio. There were ropes and pulleys rigged to sandbags. From up there he could see everything. Manny jumped behind the lens and manned the television camera. Jordan and Quincy grabbed two fire extinguishers from the wall. They held them at the ready in case anything went wrong.

Freddie held his breath as he watched Nina approach the monster slowly, cautiously. Walking straight up to Yapzilla seemed like a horrible idea—but it was Nina's monster, and he had to trust her.

Yapzilla turned toward Nina and let out a shriek aimed right at her face. *SCHHHHHHREEEEEECH!!!!!*

Nina didn't flinch. She just smiled at the monster, greeting her in a soft, friendly voice. "Hey there, Yapzilla. . . . My name is Nina Green and I'm here to interview you about your newfound fame. Tell me, you've caught the world's attention by screeching and setting things on fire, but let's take a moment to get to know the *real* you."

The monster stopped her fiery snorting and turned her gaze up toward the girl. She cocked her eyes curiously at Nina and then sent a little puff of smoke out of her neck mouth.

"I know it's hard being a monster," Nina continued soothingly to Yapzilla. "Everybody's always running away screaming from you. That must be hard for you."

To Freddie, Nina's tone sounded pretty fake, but

Yapzilla seemed to be loving the attention.

The monster nodded.

"Thank you for your honesty, Yapzilla."

Manny looked up at Freddie with utter amazement. "It's actually working. . . ."

And then it happened.

A little wisp of fire shot out of the monster's mouth. Nina winced back away from the snortle of fire, batting at her singed eyebrows.

"Ouch! Watch it, you freak!" she screamed, covering her face.

Yapzilla contorted both her mouths into two angry scowls.

"Boys!" Jordan shouted, gripping his fire extinguisher. "Time for plan B!"

One of Yapzilla's necks cranked back and let out a scorching ball of fire. It burned up the microphone in Nina's hand.

"Help!" Nina shouted, as the monster's hand coiled around Nina's waist and lifted her high into the rafters. The monster opened her mouths wide. Red-hot flames appeared in the back of Yapzilla's throat as she prepared to roast Nina with her blowtorch breath.

Nina let out a wild scream, squirming in Yapzilla's tight grasp. The monster squeezed Nina like an anaconda wrapped around its prey. Yapzilla stood up on her hind legs and rose past Freddie into the rafters. One of her necks ripped a hole through the ceiling, then came back down as the monster shrieked and clutched Nina even tighter.

Freddie scrambled across the metal catwalk and found a sandbag tied to a rope. He untied the bag and aimed it right at Yapzilla's foot. It fell with a whoosh just as Yapzilla was about to unleash another flash of fire breath. *WHAM!* The sandbag fell on the monster's toes and Yapzilla let out an awful screech. Nina squirmed free from the monster's grasp and fell, landing on her shrieking neck. The other neck swung in Freddie's direction, and Yapzilla's eyes zeroed in on her new target.

"Watch out, Freddie!" Manny yelled from below.

But Manny's warning came too late.

Freddie lost his balance. He fell down, down, down, but before he crashed to the floor, he was caught midair.

By Yapzilla's neck.

Now both he and Nina were latched on to each of the monster's necks, flailing up and down. Freddie held on for dear life, pressing his arms and legs into Yapzilla's neck skin like someone riding a mechanical bull for the first time.

Beneath him, Jordan bounded forward and aimed the nozzle of a fire extinguisher up at Yapzilla's mouth. He shot the white chemical froth down the monster's throat. Yapzilla choked and screeched once more, splatter painting the TV studio with white foam.

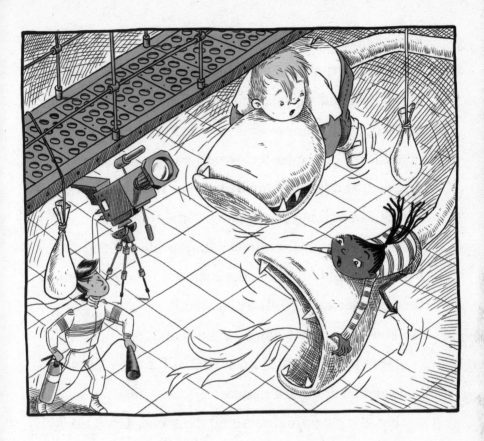

Quincy stepped up next, ready to blast the monster, too.

But before he had the chance, Nina jumped off and swung up onto the metal walkway like a gymnast on the uneven bars.

Freddie gaped as the screeching monster blew flames up at Nina.

On the walkway, Nina crawled on her hands and

knees beneath the fire blast, reaching for another sand-bag. With a grunt, she pulled the rope, dropping the sack of sand, and hit Yapzilla right on top of the hair-covered hump of her back.

ERRRK! the monster screeched. Her other neck dropped, and Freddie tumbled to the floor with a loud smack. Nina climbed back down to the stage.

Stunned from the direct hit, Yapzilla flopped her necks from side to side. She knocked over a camera, then plopped to the floor with a thunk.

The monster was down for the count.

"Way to go, fellas!" Jordan said as the fires Yapzilla had set died down to a sizzle.

Freddie got up and surveyed the scene. Thick black camera wires were tangled everywhere.

He picked up a wire and tugged on it. It seemed pretty strong. "Guys, I think we can use these cords to tie her up."

"Good idea," said Manny as he gathered up a hand-ful. "That should stop her for a while. Then we can go after Mega-Q."

The boys put down their fire extinguishers, and Quincy showed them a fancy knot he'd also learned at science camp that he guaranteed would hold.

Nina peered into a TV monitor, taking a look at her charbroiled eyebrow. "She burned off my eyebrow! I look ridiculous!"

"No one's arguing with you there . . . ," Jordan told her.

"I think it looks kind of cool," Freddie said. "Like you're the action hero in a monster movie."

"Thank you, Freddie!" she said.

"More like the monster in a monster movie." Quincy snickered.

Nina glared at Quincy as Freddie and Manny finished tying the cable cords around the monster's twin pout.

"Boom! Done!" Manny and Freddie gave each other a fist bump, and they all headed for the doorway.

"Let's blow this Popsicle stand," Nina said, leading the way out of the TV station.

It was early afternoon, but the dark heavy sky

made it feel like the sun had just set. As the kids took in the scene, they stopped their high-fiving celebration immediately. Their town looked even worse than it had before.

Smoke wafted skyward from the stores blazing on Main Street. The blare of car horns and rumble of engines from the traffic jam on the nearby highway filled the air. Sirens wailed in the distance. A shriek rang out from who knows where. Ash drifted and fluttered down from the clouds. The ground jumped with spark-ing power lines, which had been snipped into a million little pieces.

It was a full-blown symphony of chaos.

And Mega-Q was the conductor.

"My monster's the only one left," said Quincy, taking in the chaos around them. Clearly he'd done the most damage. "I'm trying to think where he would be. . . ."

"We know he's knocked out all the phone lines and the cell phone tower. He's disabled most of the town's power . . . ," Freddie said. "If you were Mega-Q, where would you go next?"

Quincy fiddled with his glasses, pacing back and forth. He stopped and put his finger in the air like he had something, then let his arm fall as the idea fizzled. "Not quite . . . just have to keep thinking."

So the know-it-all doesn't know at all, Freddie thought. Although if there was one thing he wanted Quincy to figure out, it was this.

"Come on, man," Jordan said. "Think like the mon-ster!"

"Yeah," said Nina. "What would you want if you were a monster?"

"How am I supposed to know what a monster wants? It's a monster!" Quincy snapped.

"Yeah," Nina said, "but it's based on you and what you want. Jordan loves sports, so Kraydon went to the gym. Yapzilla wanted to be famous, like me. . . ." She flicked her hair.

Quincy glanced up with the look of a detective getting a genius idea. "We have to go back to school!"

"Dude, I know you love school and all," Jordan said, "but we've got one more monster on the loose. . . ."

"Exactly. And I know my monster. I know he's smart, and I know he knows that the one thing more terrifying than one monster—" Quincy paused, raising one eyebrow dramatically.

"Is an army of monsters," Freddie finished, realizing where the mega-nerd was going with this.

"Precisely." Quincy nodded. "The only way to make more monsters is that 3D printer at school."

The kids' faces fell as they thought about what that could mean. A whole monster army to stop? That sounded like the worst thing imaginable.

"Huh, well I expect nothing less from an evil super-genius," said Manny.

"We better get to Mr. Snoozer's office, and fast," said Freddie.

The kids hopped on their bikes and hurried back to school. Freddie crossed his fingers as they rode after Quincy, wishing that the know-it-all was wrong for once in his life.

The kids snuck past their half-demolished school. Kraydon was still trapped in the soccer nets and hardened
mud. His eye went wild when he saw the kids, but he
couldn't hurt them from his rock-solid prison.

They crept around the corner and along the side of
the building. When they reached Mr. Snoozer's office,
they stopped and peeked over the windowsill. Sure
enough, through the window, they glimpsed Mega-Q
lurking around the computer and 3D printer. The monster was about the size and length of a roller-coaster car.
And he was super angry, throwing chairs and flipping
tables in some kind of tantrum.

"Get down!" Freddie yelled as Mega-Q's head jerked toward the window.

They all ducked.

"Good thinking, Q-man," Freddie told Quincy. "Way to know your monster."

"Did he see us?" Manny asked, huffing and puffing with panic.

"I don't think so," Freddie said hopefully.

Nina reached into her backpack and pulled out a black stick that looked like a small baton. She extended it out and clamped her phone to it.

"What's that?" Freddie asked.

"It's my selfie stick," she said, raising the phone's lens just over the sill so they could get a look inside.

Mega-Q was now working at the computer, his blue band of electricity squiggling around the monitor like it could control the device through some kind of power signal. They watched in horror as the monster tried to print his own monsters. He wasn't having much luck.

There were discarded gobs of pink goo everywhere. Ugly, faceless blobs—more like newborn gerbils than monsters. Freddie watched the pudgy little furless mini-monsters squiggling around. They looked disgusting.

Inside, Mega-Q slammed his talons against the printer. The printer spat out the next blob, but it was nothing like Freddie's monsters.

"This is great," Nina said excitedly. "He can't make them on his own!"

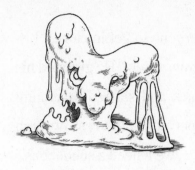

"Yeah," said Quincy. "But he'll figure it out eventually."

"What makes you so sure?" Jordan asked.

"He already knows how to use the 3D printer," said Quincy. "It's only a matter of time before he figures it out. We have to stop him now."

"How are we going to get in there and stop him?" Nina asked.

"I'll go," Freddie volunteered, not quite believing the words coming out of his mouth. "I have an idea that just might work."

"You're not going anywhere alone with Mega-Q," Manny said. "That thing is insane!"

"I drew these monsters. It's my responsibility to put an end to this," Freddie said. "I could make him an offer he can't refuse—I'll say I ditched you guys and I want to draw his monster army. He can't say no to that."

Quincy pinched his chin, thinking. "That's not a bad idea, actually."

Freddie motioned for everyone to get in close. "Listen up . . . here's what we're going to do." He grabbed his sketchbook from his backpack and started scribbling a diagram on a piece of paper while the rest of them watched. "The only thing is . . . we'll need a school bus."

"This day keeps getting crazier and crazier." Nina sighed.

After some time, the kids regrouped with everything they needed. Jordan had found the keys to the one remaining school bus tucked under the driver's seat. Manny gathered up a couple of mops from the janitor's closet that they could use like swords.

As everybody checked their walkie-talkies, Quincy turned to Freddie. "So you're going to enter the office and try to stall Mega-Q as best you can." He then turned to Nina and Jordan. "You two are in charge of the bus. We need it backed up to the exit door on the east side of the building."

"Umm," Nina said. "I'm in sixth grade. I don't drive buses. I don't even like riding in them."

"My dad drives a truck," Jordan said. "I've seen him

do it a thousand times."

"Okay then," Quincy continued. "While they're doing that, Manny and I will sneak into the building and be backup, waiting until Freddie lures Mega-Q through the door and into the bus."

Quincy clapped his hands together. "Okay, people, let's get moving."

They broke. Freddie rubbed his hands nervously. The plan would work. It had to work. If it didn't, Mega-Q was going to keep getting smarter and smarter. Soon enough, he'd be able to build an army on his own and they'd all be goners. And it would all be Freddie's fault.

"You okay, buddy?" Manny asked Freddie as they crept back toward the side door.

"Yeah, I just want this to be over and done with . . . ," Freddie said.

"Take it easy," Manny said. "Everything's going to be fine." Manny was a good liar. He handed Freddie his phone and clicked it on to video. "Here, get some more shots for the movie. It'll take your mind off what you're actually doing."

"We're not making a movie right now, Manny,"

Freddie said. "We're trying to save our town from the monsters."

"You're a smart guy," Manny said. "You can do two things at once."

"Are you kidding me?" Jordan said. "He can't even walk and chew gum at the same time."

Freddie glared at Jordan.

"I'm sorry. I take it back," Jordan said. "You're gonna do great!"

An uncomfortable silence fell over the outside of the school. Freddie looked through the window, but he couldn't see Mega-Q in the art room anymore. "Where'd he go?" Freddie peered over the windowsill, stretching his gaze this way and that. The millipede monster wasn't in Snoozer's office either.

Suddenly, the sound of a thousand legs clattered against the pavement. Freddie whirled around as Mega-Q skittered toward them in an inhuman blur. Freddie barely had time to flinch before the monster stopped just inches from his face. Mega-Q was looking right at him, cocking his bug head like he was processing a million thoughts at once.

But Freddie only had one thought going through his mind: *uh-oh*.

The monster wheeled around and shot blue sparks at the other kids. Manny, Nina, Quincy, and Jordan all backed away. Freddie had to think fast if he wanted to save his friends.

He knew what he had to do.

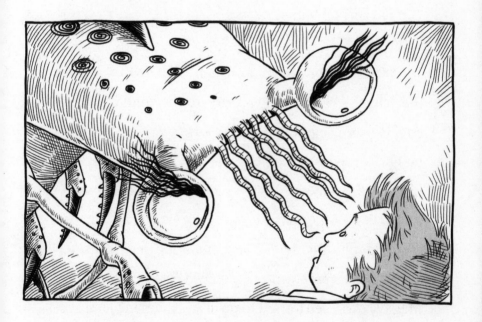

"Get out of here!" Freddie shouted at his friends.

He couldn't underestimate Mega-Q's intellect. He had to play this just right for any of it to work. He turned to Mega-Q.

"Listen, Mega-Q, those kids aren't really my friends. They were just using me. I want to work with you! We can create an army together."

Mega-Q couldn't talk, but Freddie had a sense he understood. This was either going to be his best idea ever—or the biggest mistake of his life.

In a flash, the monster grabbed Freddie and whisked him off his feet. *Mega-Q was stronger than he looked,* Freddie thought, impressed. Freddie hadn't been picked up like that since he was a little kid.

The monster carried Freddie into the art room and dropped him next to the computer in Snoozer's office. Up close, Freddie could see just how sharp each of Mega-Q's legs were, like a hundred samurai swords clacking and scratching.

On the computer screen, he saw the beginnings of the monsters Mega-Q had tried to design. They were awful looking, all out of proportion with mouths and eyes on opposite sides of their blob bodies. Freddie had done better artwork in kindergarten. The monster may be a genius, but he was no artist.

Mega-Q clicked his legs impatiently at Freddie.

"I want to help you," Freddie said. "If you want an army of minion clones, we'll give you an army of minion clones. You want flying monsters, we'll give you flying monsters." Freddie pulled up the Sculptris computer program and started clicking and sketching out a fleet of winged gargoyles and a battalion of little Mega-Q clones. His quick drawings were a million times better than Mega-Q's.

Mega-Q chittered creepily. He seemed to nod. He almost looked . . . pleased.

"I'll work for you, but on one condition. You have to let me be your second in command," Freddie said, keeping up the act.

Mega-Q tapped his legs as if he were thinking long and hard. Time was moving slower than a turtle surfing a wave of molasses. Freddie didn't know what to do next. He was worried about his town. He was worried about his dad, and his friends and classmates. The fate of everyone and everything was resting on his shoulders. And he wasn't sure he could stand it all.

"Well?" Freddie asked.

Mega-Q chittered and nodded, then lifted his front arm. Freddie put out his hand to shake on the deal. Mega-Q swatted his hand away and pointed to the art pad and pen on the table. Freddie looked meekly at the monster and gulped awkwardly. He'd gotten his friends into this mess, now he'd have to get them out. He sat down and got to work.

After a few torturous minutes, Mega-Q was starting to get antsy. Freddie looked up as he put pen to paper. "This might take a while."

Mega-Q didn't like that one bit. He started pacing the classroom on his razor-sharp legs. Freddie could barely concentrate. Freddie turned to the monster. "Hey," he said, "think I can get a bathroom break?"

Mega-Q shook his head.

"What about a snack?" he asked. "A big guy like me needs to eat. Can I go to the vending machine to get a

snack? You could come with me."

Mega-Q scowled at him, and an angry blue-white squiggle of electricity zapped between the nodes on the monster's head.

Suddenly a distinct clattering sound echoed down the hall. The millimonster's head whipped around, and he skittered out of the room to investigate the sound. The lock clicked shut on the door.

Freddie was trapped. How was he supposed to lure Mega-Q anywhere when he was locked in the room?

He looked around. There was no way he was fitting through the windows. He could break them if he had to,

but that would only botch the plan.

A shrill shriek rang out from the hallway. Freddie tensed up. It must be one of his friends. *Friends?* Freddie thought. Up to this point he had had only one friend, Manny. *Were Jordan, Nina, and Quincy really his friends?*

Another scream sounded through the door.

Whoever it was, Freddie had to help them. Mega-Q could be slicing and dicing them this very second.

He started pounding on the door with both hands. "You guys, he's coming for you! Look out, he's coming for you!"

Nothing.

Freddie crouched down and inspected the little screws of the door lock.

All he needed was a flat-head screwdriver. He riffled the room, searching through drawers and under cabinets until he found Snoozer's toolbox.

Quickly, Freddie crouched next to the door and used the screwdriver to dismantle the lock. He got the screws out, but the panel wouldn't pop off. He found a paper clip on the floor and attempted to pick the lock.

No luck.

Freddie stood up. For the first time in his life he realized his size might be a good thing. Maybe he was a freak, but he was a freak with big legs and feet who could kick hard. How strong could the door lock really be?

He lifted his leg high and brought the sole of his sneaker down on the door handle.

BAM! BAM! KERWHAM!

The door flew open.

At the end of the hallway, Mega-Q snaked around the corner, chasing Manny and Quincy. Both boys looked completely ridiculous. They were carrying mops and sporting metal buckets on their heads like helmets.

"This way!" Freddie yelled at his friends.

The millipede monster scaled the walls and spiraled up onto the ceiling as he chased them.

Freddie shoved Manny and Quincy into the art room.

Mega-Q dropped off the ceiling and slammed into the classroom door, just as Freddie pulled it shut.

Manny and Quincy gasped for breath, their backs to the door.

"Sneak attack backup did not go as planned. . . ." Manny huffed and puffed.

"That was not exactly a stealth mission, you guys," Freddie said. "We could hear you clattering around all the way down the hall!"

"It was his fault," Quincy said. "He bumped into me!"

"Did not!" Manny shouted.

"Shhhhh!" Freddie said, holding his finger to his lips.

Quincy pressed the orange button on his walkie-talkie. "Nina, Jordan, come in. . . . Over!"

Nina's voice came on the speaker. "What's the dealio? Over."

"The dealio's off," said Quincy. "New dealio. We're trapped in the art room! Come and get us. . . ."

"We're on the . . . come and getcha . . ." Nina's voice crackled with static and cut off. "Over and out . . ."

KACHUNK! One of Mega-Q's katana-blade legs exploded through the door, right between Quincy and Manny. The two boys jumped out of the way. Manny jabbed his mop at the monster's legs that were slashing through the wood. Quincy hid under a chair. Mega-Q's body hammered into the door and the top hinge popped off the frame.

"Please, oh please, just make it all stop. I'll do anything. I'll be good. I'll never be mean to either of you ever again—just make it stop!" Quincy wailed like a baby.

Mega-Q was slowly chipping away at the wood with his razor-sharp legs. Freddie pushed the art table across the floor and blocked the door with it.

Quincy's walkie-talkie

buzzed. It was Nina, shouting on the other end.

"Get out of the way," she said, her voice slightly drowned out by the roar of an engine. "We're coming through! This is plan B!"

"Hurry!" Quincy wailed, sniveling.

A school bus honked and Freddie spun around. He looked out the art room window. The bus was backing up, reversing at full speed right toward the outside wall of the building.

Beep-boop-beep-boop!

"Look out!" Freddie shouted as the bus slammed through the brick wall and stopped half in, half out of the classroom. *CRASH!*

Scratch-scratch-crack-whack-kthunk! Mega-Q's legs hacked through the classroom door.

Freddie flung open the back exit of the school bus and hopped in.

"Get in!" Freddie yelled, a hand outstretched to Quincy and Manny. "Come on, *ooph* . . . there we go, *ooph* . . . !" he grunted, pulling them both up onto the bus.

Mega-Q burst through the classroom door and violently knocked the art table across the room.

"Go!" Freddie yelled to the front of the bus. "Now!"

The wheels on the bus spun round and round, kicking up debris. Freddie tried to close the bus door, but it was too late. Mega-Q skittered across the art room and leaped onto the back of the bus, clinging to the rear bumper.

"Yo, yo, yo!" Manny shouted as the bus sped up. "Go, go, go!"

Freddie, Manny, and Quincy hustled down the aisle, away from Mega-Q. The millipede monster squiggled his legs inside the bus and squirmed toward them.

Jordan swerved the bus, and everyone jerked to the side.

Freddie's head slammed into the window. He grabbed his skull as the bus bounced over a bump.

"Up there!" Manny shouted. There was a small emergency exit right above Freddie's head!

Quincy stood on the seat, trying to open it, but he couldn't reach.

Mega-Q lunged and thrashed at the kids. His sharp legs ripped and tore through the seats as he closed in on the boys.

Freddie reached up and yanked on the lever. But it wouldn't budge.

"It's stuck!" he called.

Mega-Q let out an eardrum-rattling hiss.

"Come on, Freddie!" Nina shouted.

"Give it some elbow grease!" Jordan hollered from the driver's seat.

Freddie yanked the lever with all his might. Finally, the lever gave way and the hatch popped open with a clank.

Freddie bent down to give the two smaller boys a boost. First Manny, then Quincy stepped into the cradle of Freddie's interlocked fingers. Freddie flung them both up through the hatch as Mega-Q stretched his two front arms, grabbing for Freddie's feet. Freddie jumped onto the seat and hoisted himself through the exit. He slammed it shut behind him.

"Stop!" Manny screamed as the three boys clung to

the roof of the moving bus. Jordan hit the brakes, and the bus jerked to a halt. Jordan and Nina leaped out of the front exit and slammed the door closed.

"Gotcha sucker!" Manny hooted and hollered. "Woo-hoo!"

Mega-Q was trapped.

Freddie couldn't believe it. They had actually won!

Freddie dropped down from the top of the bus. Mega-Q bashed and clashed and battered around inside. Then something wet landed on the tip of Freddie's nose. Freddie stuck out his palm. "Do you feel that?"

"Feel what?"

"I felt it, too . . . ," said Nina, holding out an upturned hand.

"That's *no bueno*," Manny said.

"It can't be raining! These things grow in the water!" Quincy said. "We won't stand a chance!"

"I don't know how much longer this bus is gonna hold Mega-Q either," said Freddie. "If we're going to take these monsters down for good, we're going to have to fight fire with fire."

"Don't you mean monsters with monsters?" Jordan said.

"Exactly," Freddie said. "The only way to get out of this mess is to make more monsters!"

EEEEEEEEEE! Yapzilla's head-splitting screech carried on the warm desert wind and the bank of dark storm clouds that had gathered over their town.

The five of them hurried back to the demolished art room, jumping through the giant hole in the wall they'd made with the school bus. Freddie took a seat at the big art table. He cleared off Mega-Q's failed monster blobs and cracked his knuckles.

"What kind of monster are we going to make?" Quincy asked.

"We already made monsters for you three, so how about we make monsters for me and Freddie?" Manny asked.

"Good idea," Freddie agreed.

"Awesome!" Manny smiled. "Can we make one for

me that's super huge?" Manny asked. "I'm going to name him Humongotron."

Freddie was feeling jittery. There was too much pressure. When he drew the monsters based on the bullies, he had been so mad they just came pouring out of him. Now, as he tried to design a hero monster, his hands were shaking and his palms were sweating. He thought about all the people who were scared to death right now. All he wanted was for things to go back to normal. Even if that meant he had to get bullied for the rest of his life, he didn't care. He would do it in a heartbeat.

And then, just like that, Freddie started to draw.

He sketched as quickly as he could.

Humongotron had two swoops of hair for ears that could double as extra arms to grab things. A little Mohawk of hair ran over his head and he stood on a pair of birdlike feet. His mouth was lined with rows of sharp

little teeth. He had shiny smooth light-blue skin. The monster looked ferocious but kind of cute, Freddie thought.

Manny booted up the 3D printing program, while Freddie racked his brain for his monster. But nothing came to mind; panic set in again.

"What's the matter?" Manny asked, getting ready to print Humongotron.

"I can't think of anything," he said. "I have . . . artist's block."

"Here." Jordan brought over the canvas with Freddie's monster self-portrait on it, the one Jordan had shot a spitball at earlier. "Use this dude . . ."

"Oddo . . ." Freddie smiled and took the painting from his former

nemesis. "Good thinking!"

"Oddo and Humongotron," Nina said with a smile. "I like it!"

Freddie drew from the self-portrait he had done in class. Freddie's monster, Oddo, had two eyes sticking out from a round furry face. There were two horns sticking out of his head and little tusks coming out of his fluffy muzzle. Its body was covered in green fire-resistant fur. He had three arms and two fat kangaroo legs that he bounced around on and he sometimes used his arms to walk. Freddie scribbled down the powers of his and Manny's monsters.

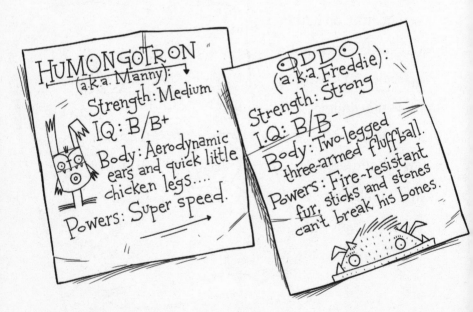

HUMONGOTRON
(a.k.a. Manny):
Strength: Medium
IQ: B/B+
Body: Aerodynamic ears and quick little chicken legs....
Powers: Super speed.

ODDO
(a.k.a. Freddie):
Strength: Strong
I.Q: B/B-
Body: Two-legged three-armed fluffball.
Powers: Fire-resistant fur, sticks and stones can't break his bones.

Just then, a crack of thunder rumbled and the sky opened up with a flash of lightning. Bullets of hard rain streaked down from the clouds. *Of all the days this dry dustbowl of a town has a thunderstorm*, Freddie thought, *it had to be today.*

Another thundercrack rumbled in the distance. Way off, Yapzilla's screech pierced the air.

"She must've gotten loose," Manny said, worry etched across his face.

From the soccer field, Kraydon wailed at the sound of Yapzilla's screech: roar, shriek, roar, shriek, almost like they were talking to each other.

Outside, the rain was coming down harder now, pouring in through the hole in the wall, puddling up on the floor. And worse, from the sound of the screeches it felt like Yapzilla was getting closer.

ROOOOOOAAAAAAARRRRRRRR! Kraydon's bellow resounded through the school. Yapzilla's piercing shriek whistled through the air.

"Hurry up, Freddie!"

"Okay, I'm done," said Freddie. "Load up the printer!"

 Manny went over to the printer. "Hand me one of those cartridges," he said to Quincy. The mega-nerd reached into one of the boxes on the shelving unit and pulled out one of the 3D printer cartridges. The pink goo inside looked like Silly Putty mixed with hair gel. "These the ones?"

"That's them," Freddie confirmed.

"Where does this stuff even come from?" Quincy asked.

"I don't know," said Freddie. "I think Mr. Snoozer said he got it from the internet."

Manny turned on the 3D printer, and Quincy loaded the cartridges into it.

Everyone watched in silence as Freddie hit print and the machine fired up. Yapzilla's screech kept getting louder and louder as the storm raged.

Their eyes were glued to the machine. The room was breathless. Freddie's stomach felt fluttery.

"Come on, come on," Freddie said as the printer

started spitting out the new monsters. Oddo printed out first, a fluff of green fur.

"Aww," Nina cooed, crouching next to Oddo. "You're kinda cute, aren't you? Weird lookin', but kind of cute."

STRREEEECCHH!!

ROWR! Oddo let out an adorable roar and then nuzzled up to Nina like a purring kitten. Oddo closed his eyes and smiled as Nina stroked his fur.

Quincy looked at the monster skeptically, then at Freddie. "That's your ferocious secret weapon?"

"What's he going to do? Snuggle the other monsters to death?" Jordan said.

"Don't listen to them. I like him, Freddie," Nina said. "He's cute and cuddly even if he's shaped a little weird."

"I told you I had to work quicker than normal," Freddie said. "But maybe once he gets big he'll be fine."

RRAAA!!

"If you say so, man," said Manny.

When Humongotron printed, Manny's monster

was the same size as Oddo. He had tiny little arms for his body and legs that coiled around like springs. He did not exactly look like a Humongotron. More like a minitron.

The strange-looking monster climbed onto Manny's lap.

Freddie smiled as the little monster nuzzled into the crook of Manny's arm. It was nice to have sweet monsters for a change. He wished he'd just made these little guys to begin with.

But Freddie knew you couldn't take back the past: all you could do was learn from your mistakes to make

138

things better in the future. Freddie pulled out his original monster drawings and showed them to Oddo and Humongotron. The blueprints for Kraydon, Yapzilla, and Mega-Q stared back at them.

"You good, them bad," Freddie said, then repeated. "You good, them bad."

The monsters looked at him, blinking blankly. He had no clue if they actually understood what he was trying to say to them.

Just then, Humongotron hopped over to the boxes on the shelf where the goo cartridges were stored. "Yum yums," he said and started picking up the little silica packets labeled DO NOT EAT from the boxes of goo. Humongotron shoveled the little packets into his mouth and started gobbling them up.

"No, no, no!" Manny said. "Spit that out!"

"Yum yums." Humongotron swallowed and then smiled at Manny. "Yum yums . . ."

"Okay, you guys," Freddie said. "We have to get these little dudes into some water so they can grow. We don't have much time."

"Just put them outside in the rain," Nina said.

"Umm, I maybe wouldn't do that . . . ," Quincy said with a twinge of fright in his voice.

"Why not?" Freddie asked, then turned his head as Quincy pointed toward the hole in the art room wall.

Through the curtain of rain, they watched in horror as the thunderstorm doused the muddy soccer field

with thick torrents of rain. Kraydon was growing even bigger. The stone cracked around his feet.

In a few seconds, he broke free.

The monstrous maelstrom was fast upon them.

Freddie and the rest of the kids rushed the baby monsters to the locker rooms and turned the showers on full blast. They then wadded up handfuls of paper towels and stuffed them down the floor drains. "We need to flood this place so our monsters can grow," Freddie explained.

Oddo grew almost immediately. He was soon about the size of a sports mascot and getting bigger.

But Humongotron wasn't changing at all.

Freddie crouched down. "What's the matter with you, buddy? You don't want to get big?"

"Yum yums," Humongotron said, because, well,

that's all Humongotron could say.

"So I guess Humongotron's a pretty stupid name for him now," Manny mumbled.

"Yeah, kinda . . ." Freddie agreed with him.

"That's okay," said Manny. "We can just shorten it to Mungo."

"Dang!" Freddie said, kicking the floor of the shower room with a splash.

"We've got other problems right now, Freddie!" Nina yelped.

She'd been keeping watch through a gaping hole in the wall of the locker room, Freddie could see the school bus flashing with Mega-Q's angry blue sparks. Beyond the curtain of falling rain, he could just make out Kraydon's and Yapzilla's figures. The thunderous stomp of the two gigantic rain-soaked monsters was getting closer.

Oddo was now almost too big for the shower room, but Mungo still wasn't growing. "They need a little more time!"

"We're out of time!" Jordan yelled.

Just as the words left his mouth, Kraydon and Yapzilla stomped up to the front of the school. The kids left their monsters in the flooded shower room and raced down the hall, to better see what they were dealing with.

Freddie gazed upon the two mammoth monsters in horror. Yapzilla was absolutely enormous, at least twice the size of her previous two-headed self. Kraydon was twice his former size, too. He towered over the school yard.

Manny, Quincy, Nina, and Jordan ran up behind Freddie. The five of them craned their necks to see the enormous monsters.

Yapzilla let out a bloodcurdling screech that shattered the glass at the front of the building. The monster's high-pitched squawk was even louder than before. Freddie felt his tummy fat jiggle with the sonic vibrations of Yapzilla's inhuman squawk.

The kids covered their ears with their headsets, but it couldn't block out the sound. Freddie fell to his knees, unable to move, pressing the padded headphones into his ears as hard as he could. He looked over at Manny, who had his eyes shut tight, clasping the headphones to the sides of his own head.

"OMG," Nina shouted. "I feel like my brain's going to explode."

"Make it stop!" Quincy cried.

Freddie could barely hear his friends' yelling over the screeching monster. He felt like his eyes were going to pop out of his skull.

Jordan ran toward a pile of rubble. He picked up a stray brick off the ground. With a loud grunt, he threw the brick into the air with all his strength.

The brick sailed up and up and up, aiming straight at Yapzilla's screeching mouth.

GULP.

Yapzilla choked, then went quiet.

Freddie dropped his hands from his ears as the shrieking finally stopped.

Yapzilla's silence, however, didn't last long. The gigantic two-mouthed beast made a gagging sound and spat out the brick like a Tic Tac. She reared her other neck mouth back and unleashed a massive rolling fireball.

"Look out!" Nina shouted at the top of her lungs as they ducked behind the wall of the school's lobby. The swath of fire lasted for a few seconds, and Freddie felt beads of sweat trickle down his face from the heat.

Then with a sudden stomp forward, Kraydon crouched low on his hind legs. He peered his spiraling Cyclops eye through the doorway and sent out a pulsating eye beam right at the kids.

"Run!" Freddie tackled Manny out of the way.

As he hit the ground, Freddie felt the pulse of the monster's eye beam. It felt ten times stronger than before. Freddie and Manny stopped, dropped, and rolled into a classroom, just out of harm's way.

A few moments later, the pulse stopped and the boys got to their feet. They looked back out into the hall and gasped. They couldn't believe their eyes.

Jordan, Nina, and Quincy were completely frozen in stone.

They stood in different action poses, caught in time as they tried to escape Kraydon's gaze.

"He's going to smash them!" Manny shouted as Kraydon raised his mammoth tail and swung for the kids.

Freddie raced into the hall, grabbing the stone Nina and dragging it into a doorway. "Come on!" he shouted to Manny. Manny sprinted after him, pulling at the Quincy statue.

Kraydon's tail smashed through the ceiling as the boys pulled Jordan's statue out of the way. With the

three bullies now frozen in stone, Freddie and Manny were on their own.

Sort of . . .

All of a sudden, the building rumbled, and the boys spun around as Oddo burst through the roof of the school.

Tiny Mungo clung to the giant fuzzball's fur.

Another screech from the giant double-mouthed freak shocked their eardrums, and the boys crumpled to the floor of the lobby.

With his ears plugged, Freddie stared up at Oddo. His monster seemed unaffected by the supersonic screech. *That's a good sign*, Freddie thought. *Oddo is working!* He had given the monster retractable ears that could open and close.

Oddo gazed down at Freddie with a sweet smile that quickly changed into an angry scowl as he focused on the monster bullies. Mungo jumped off his humongous friend and landed on the floor. The fuzzy monster stepped outside the school and bounced himself off the ground on his big belly. Oddo whirled around in the air, clocking Yapzilla across her neck with all three of his arms spinning like a pinwheel.

One mouth was silenced, but the other mouth blasted a huge stream of fire at Oddo.

"No!" Manny shrieked as the fireball consumed Oddo.

But the flames had no effect. Oddo's fur burned to a crisp and then sprouted back in a big puff almost immediately.

Now Kraydon emitted a low growl, watching the action in front of him. His eyeball swirled and shot out its energy pulse toward the two good monsters.

The giant fuzzy oddball didn't seem to notice Kraydon's eye swirling.

"Oddo!" Freddie hollered at their monster. "Get out of the way! He'll turn you into a rock!"

Kraydon's gaze zeroed in on Oddo. But when it hit him, his fur only crumbled away and then rapidly grew back in a big fluffy poof. The giant fuzzy oddball was completely unaffected by Kraydon's gaze.

Kraydon grunted and ran at Oddo with a *ROOOOOAAAAR!* He grabbed Oddo and threw him to the ground.

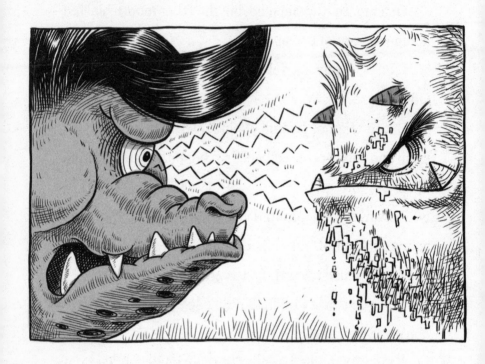

"Look out!" Freddie yelled, and bumped Manny out of the way as Kraydon's back foot came down next to his friend's head and cracked the floor.

Oddo broke free from Kraydon's clutches and used

his three arms to spring off the ground, clobbering Kraydon with a hard combo punch.

Kraydon flew back and let out a whimper as he flew out of the school, high over the playground, and landed in the parking lot. He almost hit the school bus that Mega-Q was still trapped in.

Freddie and Manny sprinted outside to watch the fight. Yapzilla charged forward to defend Kraydon, and now the three enormous monsters fought, grappling with one another, swinging their arms, rearing their necks, shooting flames, grunting, and growling. It was two against one and it was starting to look like Oddo was in trouble.

"There has to be a way to help him!" Manny shouted.

Kraydon and Yapzilla were teaming up to throttle Oddo. But something strange was happening. Oddo was bouncing right off a car, giggling like he thought it was the funniest thing in the entire world. Oddo laughed and laughed as if being hurled around by two monsters was hilarious.

That's the way, Oddo, Freddie realized. *Don't let them*

get to you. They can't hurt you if you don't let them get to you.

Strangely, Yapzilla started to giggle, too. Even Kraydon let out a deep bellowing chuckle. Oddo laughed even harder.

Suddenly it seemed like the monsters weren't trying to kill one another. It was just a big game!

"Look!" Manny pointed. "They think he's funny!"

With all three monsters laughing now, Oddo bounced up and flung himself at both Yapzilla and Kraydon. He wrapped them up in his big fluffy arms, and they rolled through the parking lot playfully, squashing cars like they were nothing.

Kraydon shucked off Oddo's headlock and threw another haymaker at Oddo's gut. The furry, three-armed monster went sailing into the school bus where Mega-Q was still stuck.

Oddo bashed into the big yellow bus and flipped it over. Inside, Mega-Q flashed electric blue and let out a hideous squawk.

And then the windshield of the bus shattered in an

explosion of thick glass bits.

Oddo climbed right back up and laughed heartily at the spill he had just taken. The big fluffy monster's chuckle bellowed through the air. Yapzilla and Kraydon fell over they were laughing so hard.

But they were also laughing so hard they didn't notice that Mega-Q had squirmed out of the busted windshield behind Oddo.

Freddie gasped as Mega-Q skittered toward his monster.

"Oddo! Watch out!" Manny cried.

Oddo spun around just as Mega-Q lunged at him.

The big, furry monster backed up quickly. Mega-Q's legs stabbed fiercely at him.

Freddie was nervous. The entire time he had been designing Oddo, he hadn't given him any defenses against Mega-Q. After all, Mega-Q had been trapped in the bus! Freddie had only been worried about Kraydon and Yapzilla.

Oddo flung his arms up in defense against Mega-Q's blade-like leg attack. The milli-monster's legs sliced gashes in Oddo's arms. The monster's fur flew off him in a flurry as Mega-Q kept coming at him.

Oddo cowered against the school building, frightened and quivering, as the milli-monster scuttled toward him.

Mega-Q pounced, fast and violent, spiraling around Oddo's body. Oddo spun and flailed, but Mega-Q's legs pinched Oddo's soft tummy, holding him in place.

For a long, sickening moment, Freddie watched in horror as the brainsect monster lifted its spindly needle-point legs and stabbed Oddo in the back.

Oddo's face went wide-eyed with surprise at the sudden pain. His mouth hung open slightly.

His eyes went blank.

Freddie's heart sank as Oddo slumped to the ground. He cringed as Mega-Q's legs slid out from Oddo's sides, dripping pink goo onto the blacktop.

He couldn't believe it. Oddo was down for the count. Jordan, Nina, and Quincy had all been turned to stone. Mega-Q was victorious.

And it was all Freddie's fault.

A pit formed in his stomach. He couldn't believe this was happening.

Kraydon and Yapzilla hung their heads, too, as they watched their new favorite monster oozing watery pink goo all over the pavement. And that's when Freddie realized: these monsters weren't *just* monsters. These monsters had feelings, too.

"Don't just stand there, get him!" Freddie cried to Yapzilla and Kraydon. He pointed at Mega-Q.

Kraydon and Yapzilla scowled and approached the evil millipede monster. He had destroyed their favorite new playmate and now he was going to pay. They both charged, taking down Mega-Q in one big tackle. The trio of monsters rumbled, rolling around in a giant blurry flurry of motion.

Yapzilla sprayed a swath of fire. Mega-Q dodged Yapzilla's flames, barrel-rolling out of the way. His electric current flashed and zapped a bolt of blue energy at Yapzilla.

BZZZZT!

The electric charge struck the two-headed monster right in her fire-breathing mouth. Yapzilla stumbled, but Kraydon was able to lumber forward and leap into the air.

Mega-Q looked up at the massive beast flying at him, and his slug eyes bugged out. At the last second,

158

Mega-Q rolled on his back and stuck up his legs.

As Kraydon's giant fist came down, Mega-Q's legs pierced the flesh between Kraydon's knuckles. The gigantic monster stumbled, yipping like a hurt puppy.

With his two mega nemeses down, Mega-Q then turned his attention toward Freddie and Manny. The boys looked at each other in panic and dashed back inside the school. Mungo raced ahead of them. But when Mungo reached the vending machine, he stopped dead in his tracks.

Manny looked down at Mungo, who was gazing at the vending machine, his mouth open, drooling onto the linoleum floor. "Yum yums . . ."

"Is that all you can think about right now?" Manny yelled, disappointed in his monster. "We're about to get killed! Help us! Do *something*!"

Mungo shot him a hurt look, his googly eyes going wide. "Yum yums," he said.

Freddie looked down at the weird little creature who wouldn't grow. Why hadn't he grown like Oddo? It didn't make sense. The little monster looked up at Freddie now. "Yum yums," Mungo said once again.

This time, though, when Mungo uttered the word *yum yums*, a lightbulb popped on in Freddie's head.

"The yum yums!" Freddie shouted at Manny.

"What about them?" Manny asked.

"That's the reason little Mungo wouldn't grow! Silica makes things dehydrate," Freddie said. "It sucks up all the water and dries everything out. That's why they must have put so many in the 3D printer cartridge boxes . . . to make sure that pink goo stuff wouldn't get all wet. . . ."

"So if we feed it to the monsters, you think they'll shrink?" Manny asked.

"Mungo did," said Freddie, pointing to the miniature monster. "He got wet and didn't grow."

"That's how we fix this! We're going to shrink them," Freddie shouted.

"But Mungo ate them all!" Manny said.

"Not all." Freddie looked up at the vending machine. Just like Jordan had said, there was the answer. Rows and rows of jerky in all three flavors.

Freddie pulled out his wallet. It was empty.

Dang!

He turned to Manny. "Do you have any money?"

"Nah, man, I'm broke right now. . . ."

Freddie clutched at his head, pacing back and forth. He looked at the slot with the flap door on the snack machine. His arm was too big to fit inside. Manny's arm was too short to grab the beef jerky. They could smash the glass, but that might make too much noise, and they didn't want to draw attention to where they were inside the building.

Then Freddie looked down at Mungo.

"Come here, little fella," he said, picking the fuzzy little monster up. "Yum yums. You get yum yums!"

He placed him in the candy slot. Mungo looked up from inside and Freddie pointed to the beef jerky, tapping on the glass. The little monster climbed up to B 2, 3, and 4 and grabbed all the jerky: teriyaki, chipotle, and original. Twenty-four bags total. Each of them contained the small pouch of silica that would save them all.

"Well," Manny said, "I guess it is pretty awesome to be small sometimes."

Freddie ripped open the packages with Manny's help. Mungo jumped down and slipped out of the vending machine.

Once they had collected all the silica packets, Freddie and Manny stuffed them in their pockets and ran outside. Mega-Q was still circling the fallen megamonsters, guarding his prey. Mungo nodded excitedly. "Yum yums?" He grabbed for the packets, but Freddie pulled them out of his reach. Mungo made a pouty face.

Freddie pointed at Mega-Q.

Mungo nodded.

Freddie pointed at Mega-Q again. "Give him yum yums. . . ."

Mungo nodded and took the armful of packets, Freddie handed him about a dozen, which was all he could carry. Mungo grinned and scarfed a yum yum.

"Mungo, wait!" Freddie said. "They ALL want yum yums. . . ."

Mungo nodded again. "Yum yums!" He popped

another silica packet into his mouth and gulped it down. "Not for you!" Freddie said as he pointed at the monsters. "For them!"

"Yum yums," Mungo said again, and took off.

Freddie turned toward Manny. "We've got to teach that little guy some new words. . . ."

The boys crept behind Mungo and got close to where the monster action was.

Kraydon and Yapzilla had gotten back on their feet and managed to get Mega-Q cornered against the school building.

Mega-Q jabbed his legs at Kraydon and Yapzilla, who managed to dodge him and keep him at bay. Kraydon roared and Yapzilla squawked and Mega-Q hissed. They couldn't hold off much longer. It was clear something was about to give.

Then, in a wild, speedy blur, Mungo came zooming from around the corner of the building. The little guy leaped into the air and chucked the silica packets into Mega-Q's mouth, like a shortstop hucking an out to first base.

Mega-Q gagged and swallowed them down with a *glug*.

Mungo then bounded off the ground again with his springy legs and did a little spin move in the air before tossing the other packets into the back of Kraydon's and then Yapzilla's throats.

An odd expression fell over the monsters' faces as the silica packets started to dissolve inside them. They didn't even realize what had hit them.

Mega-Q collapsed to the ground. His long millipede body writhed and shook. A pinkish-white froth shot out of his mouth. Mega-Q vomited and convulsed as he began to shrink. The more froth he spat up, the more he shrank. In a matter of a few minutes, he was back to the size that he was when he was first printed.

Kraydon and Yapzilla did the same, frothing and shrinking right before Freddie's eyes. Soon, all three monsters lay motionless in puddles of their own mouth foam.

"Yay-yah!" Manny shouted and gave Freddie a high five. Mungo zipped over to them, sprang off the ground,

and smacked both their hands.

"We did it!" Freddie hollered. "I can't believe it. . . ."

But their celebration ended as they ran over to Oddo, who was limp and still on the pavement. Freddie crouched down next to his monster. He put his hand on Oddo's furry arm and pet the monster. "Oddo?" he asked gently as he inspected the deep stab wound on his back.

"Is he?" Manny gulped down hard.

"He's not responding," Freddie said, a sadness

creeping into his voice. "I think Mega-Q stabbed him too deep. . . ."

"Yum yums," Mungo said.

"No, Mungo," said Freddie. "He's too hurt. He doesn't want any yum yums."

Mungo jumped onto Oddo's belly and raced up to his mouth, stuffing a packet of silica pellets into the enormous fuzzball's mouth and ramming it down his throat.

"Don't, Mungo!" Manny said. "Stop!"

"Get off him!" Freddie cried, pulling the little monster off Oddo.

Just then, Oddo's body began to shake, and the pink froth gurgled out of his mouth. The furry triple-armed monster shrank down.

Then, amazingly, Oddo's wounds began to close up and heal. Soon enough, Oddo was the size of a grapefruit. Oddo's eyes flicked open, and the shrunken monster started to giggle.

"He's alive!" Freddie picked up the tiny creature and hugged him to his chest. "He's alive!"

The rest of the shrunken monsters—Kraydon, Yapzilla, and Mega-Q—rose off the cement and stumbled over to Freddie and Manny. The boys picked up the toy-sized monsters and carried them inside the school. Through the hole in the hallway ceiling, they could see the sun break through the dark storm clouds.

Somewhere, there was a rainbow.

Freddie stopped next to the frozen statues of Jordan, Nina, and Quincy.

Freddie looked at his former enemies, but he no longer saw the kids who had bullied him and called him names. They weren't monsters. They were people. People who made mistakes. People who were mean sometimes. And maybe they deserved a detention, but they didn't deserve to be turned to stone forever.

Freddie lifted Kraydon in the palm of his hand until they were face-to-face. He stared right into the little monster's pulsating eye. "Turn them back," Freddie ordered him sternly.

Kraydon just stared at him.

"Turn them back!" Freddie wailed at the top of his lungs, but Kraydon could only look at him sheepishly.

"Freddie, chill," Manny said. "Maybe this is what happens to people when they're mean. . . ."

"No way, man," Freddie said. "I don't want this on me. And neither do you." He pointed Kraydon at the bully statues. "You did this!" he shouted at the minimonster. "Do you see what you did? You think it's okay to turn people to stone? Well, it's not! It's not okay, Kraydon. And we're not leaving here until you—"

Freddie's tirade was cut short by the sound of Kraydon sniffling. Very slowly, Kraydon's eyeball glazed over and looked like it was going to fill with tears. "It's okay," Freddie said, his voice softening. "We just want our friends back."

The little monster's eyeball began to spin, rotating in the opposite direction from usual. Kraydon emitted the pulse from its eye, aiming it at the three statues. The energy from the pulse had a warm glow and enveloped Freddie's friends. And just like that Jordan, Nina, and Quincy transformed from stone back into flesh and blood.

Their human selves gasped for air. They looked at Freddie and Manny and Kraydon and the rest of their tiny monsters. "What's going on? Is this a dream?" Nina asked, groggy eyed, rubbing her face.

"No dream," Manny said, handing her mini Yapzilla. "Completely real monsters."

"What happened to them?" Jordan and Quincy both asked at the exact same time.

"This little guy." Manny picked Mungo off the floor and held him up. "We got more silica from the beef jerky in the vending machine and Mungo fed it to the monsters when they were all fighting because Mega-Q hurt Oddo, except not really because when we shrunk him down, he was okay. . . ." Manny gasped for air.

"We'll just see it when the movie comes out," Quincy said.

Nina giggled as Yapzilla nuzzled into her arms.

Mega-Q slithered up Quincy's pant leg, and Quincy started squirming and even laughed a little until his monster came out his shirt collar and perched on his shoulder.

Jordan lifted Kraydon and placed him in the pocket of his varsity jacket.

Freddie and Manny let Oddo and Mungo sit on their shoulders.

"You really came through in the clutch, Freddie,"

Quincy said, like he read Freddie's mind.

"Yeah, for real," Nina said. She went up to Freddie and gave him a big hug.

"Thanks, guys," said Freddie. "I was just trying to get us out of the mess I got us into in the first place."

"Nice work, brother! Way to go!" Jordan high-fived Freddie.

"Okay . . . okay," Manny said jokingly. "Just remember he was my friend first."

Freddie looked at the four of them and smiled. He couldn't believe that earlier today, he couldn't stand these three people. And now they were actually friends. It was almost as crazy as a bunch of 3D-printed monsters coming to life.

Almost.

They still had some business to attend to.

"We have to make sure this doesn't happen again . . . ," Freddie said, heading back to the art room.

"What are we doing?" Nina asked as she and the others trailed behind Freddie.

"I'm going to destroy the printer," Freddie said, a steely look of determination glinting in his eyes.

"But we haven't even gotten a chance to study it to figure out how it made real monsters!" Quincy said. "You can't do that!"

"Watch me . . . ," Freddie said as they approached the art room.

"Whoa!" Manny called out in surprise. The five of them came to a sudden stop. A massive fleshy blob was blocking the doorway and squishing out into the hall. It looked like a humongous piece of bubble gum. Freddie could barely see around it. What little he could see was disturbing, to say the least. The rest of the art room was filled to the brim with Mega-Q's waterlogged blob spawn. Mega-Q made a gleeful chirping

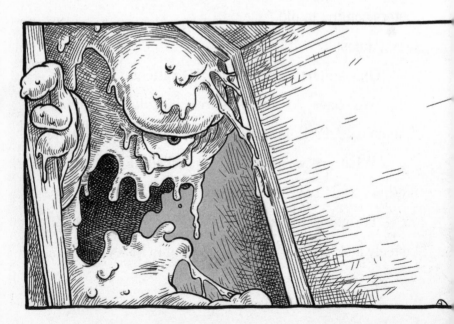

noise when he saw his army.

"Nuh-uh," Manny said to the little milli-monster. "Not cool."

"The rain must have gotten inside and made them huge!" Freddie yelped. The blobs were seeping out through the windows and the gaping hole in the wall made by the bus.

"They're getting out!" Freddie shouted. "Come on!"

The kids all hustled outside.

The last of the storm clouds passed above them and only a hint of sunshine remained, peeking through for a moment to cast an eerie low lighting over the scene.

There were five blobs total, each one bigger than the

next, growing superfast as they squished and squelched out of the art room and soaked in puddles on the parking lot. Some of them didn't even have eyes or faces, just mouths. They looked like enormous slugs.

Freddie and his friends watched in horror as the blobs rose up to enormous heights. Manny's chin pointed straight up in the air as he gazed at the mindless giants that Mega-Q's blob monsters had become.

"Aw, man," Manny said. "Not again . . ."

Quickly, Freddie dug around in his pocket. He had only twelve silica packets left. That meant about two per monster. He hoped it would be enough.

"Come on, you guys!" Freddie passed out two packets to everyone: Manny, Jordan, Nina, and Quincy. Mungo and Oddo took off with a packet each, and in no time, they'd climbed up two of the blobs, scaling their gooey flanks. The two monsters held on tightly to the silica packets as they worked their way up the slope of the blobs' bulbous bodies.

Jordan started running around the third blob with Kraydon riding on his back. The little monster's eye swirled and shot his eye beam at the foot of the mammoth blob.

The pinkish flesh hardened into stone, and the glob monster stopped in its tracks, unable to drag its cement body any farther.

Meanwhile, Nina dashed back through the hole in the art room wall. She grabbed a spray can of fixative off the storage shelf and ran back outside. She sprinted toward the fourth blob and sprayed the flammable liquid around the base of the blob.

"Come on, girl!" she shouted to Yapzilla on her shoulder. "Let 'em have it!"

She dropped Yapzilla on the ground, and the tiny two-headed monster galloped up to the massive blob. Yapzilla unleashed a torrent of streaming fire.

In a bright flash, the blob went up in flames. As the thing burned up, it didn't even shriek or make any kind of noise. It just sunk to the blacktop in an icky pink puddle.

The next blob over, Manny was yelling at Mungo, directing the little guy at the monster's blobby mouth.

The fifth blob moved toward Quincy and Mega-Q.

"Zap it, Mega!" Quincy ordered. Mega-Q looked like he wasn't going to obey, but then, right as the blob was about to pass through a puddle, Mega-Q shot a blue volt of monster energy at the rainwater.

The blob flew back in shock, jiggling back and forth like a Jell-O mold. And it seemed like they got him, but as he toppled, he fell onto Manny. The blob gulped him

up with a glug-gluggle, and Freddie watched in horror as his friend became encased in the blob monster's
blubber.

Manny mouthed the words: "I can't breathe!" He
desperately tried to claw his way out.

Freddie ran over to the blob and jumped on it with a

squelching splat. He jammed his arm into its misshapen
mouth, and dropped a silica packet inside the thing's
middle. His arm made a suction-cup pop as he pulled
his arm out of the monster. He watched victoriously as

the blob convulsed and shrank into a mushy puddle.

As it rolled over, Manny wrenched his way out of the monster. He fell onto his butt, gasping for air, covered in sludge.

"You okay, Manny?" Freddie asked.

Between coughs, Manny was able to talk. "Yeah . . . I'm good. . . ."

As Manny recovered, Jordan threw more packets into a blob's mouth hole. Mungo followed Jordan's lead and fired the packet of pellets into another monster's blob mouth. Oddo plunged one of his arms into the last blob's boneless bod and released the silica.

All was quiet, and in a matter of minutes, all the blobs had melted into the ground.

"We did it, you guys!" Freddie shouted. But he was cut off by the wail of a siren and the grumble of a car engine in the distance. A pair of helicopters chopped through the clouds, shining two spotlights on the ground below.

A caravan of cars, police cruisers, and three news vans were headed straight for the school.

"Oh, now they send us some backup!" Manny grumbled with sarcasm.

"We have to hide these little guys!" Freddie said, gesturing to the monsters.

"He's right—we can't let anyone know we have the monsters," said Quincy.

"Okay, monsters, listen up!" Nina said. "Nobody can know about you, so we're going to put you away for a little, and it's really important that you be quiet . . . that means no roaring or shrieking or fire breathing or electric blue spark things or saying 'yum yums' or anything else, for that matter, that's going to get us in trouble with the grown-ups. You'll learn about them later. They're a real pain in the you know what. So just chill out and everything will be cool, *capiche*?"

The monsters stared at her blankly.

"*Capiche?*" she shouted at them, and the monsters blinked and nodded.

They each put their monsters away in their backpacks.

The cars were getting closer, but Freddie had one

more job before he faced the music. Quickly, without anyone noticing him go, Freddie ducked back into the art room and into Snoozer's office. He picked up the 3D printer and raced down the hallway. He stopped at his locker and opened the lock as fast as he could, then he placed the 3D printer at the base of the locker, covering it with old homework assignments and draping an XXL T-shirt over it. They'd have to figure out

what to do with it later. Nothing good would come from leaving it out for anyone to see—he knew that for a fact.

Freddie raced back to his friends as the cars drew closer to the school.

The cars slowed to a standstill, idling in the school parking lot. Cops, cameramen, and reporters jumped out of the cars and surrounded the kids.

Nina's eyes lit up when she saw the TV cameras. She stepped toward the bright light of the reporters like a moth to a flame.

Freddie yanked her back by the shoulder. "No way," he said. "None of us can talk to anybody about this. Not even if it gets us on TV."

Nina snapped out of it. "Of course! You're right. We have to protect our new little monster pets."

"Exactly," Freddie said.

"Whoa, check it out," Quincy said, pointing to the crowd of people heading their way. "That's the sheriff and the mayor. And that's Councilman Rodriguez, and that's the school superintendent."

"How do you know who all those people are?" Jordan asked him.

"I watch a lot of government access," Quincy said, and Jordan shot him a funny look. "I'm into local politics—so what?"

"We're so going to get busted for this," Manny said.

"No, we're not," said Freddie. "Not if we stick together. As long as we keep our mouths shut, we'll be able to keep our monsters. That's what everyone wants, right?"

They all nodded.

"We have to make a pact," Freddie said.

"Group pinky swear," said Manny.

They stood in a circle and held out their hands. The five kids locked their pinky fingers with those of the person next to them until the circle was complete.

Freddie looked up as the crowd of people approached the school and surrounded them. At the front of the group, Freddie spotted his dad hustling toward him.

"Freddie! I was so worried!" Mr. Liddle wrapped his arms around his son and gave him a big hug. "I couldn't find you, and when they told me you didn't evacuate with the rest of the school, I thought I'd lost you, but we started a search party! Are you and your friends okay?"

"They're not really my fr—" Freddie started to say when Jordan, Nina, and Quincy jumped in.

"Yes . . . we are," they all said at once.

Suddenly the rest of their parents pushed through the crowd and reunited with their kids.

Mr. Liddle smiled up at his son and down at Freddie's friends. Then he looked around, confused. "Are the monsters still on the loose?"

"It's okay," Freddie said. "The giant monsters are gone. . . ." *Which*, Freddie thought, *wasn't technically a lie*. The *giant* monsters were gone. Now the only monsters around were the ones that fit in their backpacks.

Reporters and police began to swarm the kids, firing questions at them in rapid succession.

"Did you see what they were?" one of the reporters shouted.

"What happened to them?"

"Where did they come from?"

"Where did they go?"

Freddie didn't know what to say. "Ummmm . . ." was all he could muster.

The rest of the kids didn't do any better. Except for Nina, who stepped right up into the limelight of the cameras. "It was just so, so scary," she said, stammering a little, her eyes filling with fake tears. "We don't know what happened. We were just trying not to get killed!" She paused and gasped, pretending to cry.

She's not bad, Freddie thought, watching Nina's performance.

"No more questions!" her father shouted at the reporters. "Can't you see our kids have been through enough for today?"

As their parents shooed away the news cameras, Freddie noticed Manny's backpack wriggle slightly and then settle down. The little monsters stayed quiet, not making a peep.

He smiled to himself, standing in the glare of the late afternoon sunlight.

The black clouds from the storm had drifted away to the horizon. He looked up in the sky and caught a glimpse of a rainbow arching overhead.

Maybe everything is going to be okay, Freddie thought.

At least for a little while anyway.

Acknowledgments

I would like to offer many Gargantuan thanks to the following people: Hayley Wagreich, Sara Shandler, Josh Bank, and Les Morgenstein for their mega-brained efforts in helping me conceive this idea and bring this whopper to 3D life; Alice Jerman and Emilia Rhodes for their ginormous contributions in growing this book from a tiny creature into a fully fleshed-out behemoth; and Ryan Harbage for his colossal counsel and assistance along the monster-ridden way.

The action continues in

The only thing worse than monsters? Bugs. Billions of them.

Just when Freddie Liddle thought he could catch a break, a new kind of terror infests his town: slimy, disgusting, man-eating, self-replicating bugs. But these aren't just any pests—these bugs were 3D printed by Freddie's classmate Trevor, and they're stronger, faster, and meaner than any other insect on earth.

Now it's up to Freddie, his new friends, and their pet monsters to stop these bad bugs before they devour everything in sight. The kids start crunching, stomping, and smashing, but as the bugs get bigger, the chances of winning against them get smaller. Can Freddie and his friends get the creepy crawlers to buzz off before their town goes *SPLAT*?

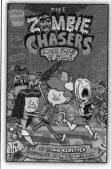